A DEADLY
SICKNESS

A DEADLY SICKNESS

John Penn

CHARLES SCRIBNER'S SONS

New York

Copyright © 1985 John Penn

Library of Congress Cataloging in Publication Data
Penn, John.
   A deadly sickness.
   I. Title.
PR6066.E496D3   1985   823'.914   85-14268
ISBN 0-684-18464-8

1 3 5 7 9 11 13 15 17 19   F/C   20 18 16 14 12 10 8 6 4 2

Printed in the United States of America.

Part One

CHAPTER 1

It was many years since the large double bed had felt a woman's weight, and now Sir Oliver Poston lay alone in the middle of it. His wife had died in childbirth when Alan, his only son, was born. It was mainly for her sake, he thought as he drifted in and out of consciousness, that he had always done his best for Alan, however difficult and unrewarding the effort might have sometimes seemed.

He groaned softly as he shifted in the bed, and his white hands fluttered on the coverlet. His sight had been failing for some months, but his eyes opened for a moment. His manservant, Tom Calindar, threw the doctor a quick, anxious glance. Dick Band picked up his black bag. He had given the old man yet another injection to ease the pain and help him sleep, and there was nothing further that he or anyone else could do.

The doctor shook his head. 'No,' he said to Tom, as he had done so many times over the past year. 'There's no immediate danger, as far as I can see. Sir Oliver won't go tonight, nor tomorrow, nor this week. But, after that, who knows? He may last a month, even a few months—or he may not.' The only certainty, he added to himself, was that the end wouldn't be very long in coming. Tom responded with a sad nod.

Sir Oliver's taste hadn't run to ostentatious luxury, but the bedroom was spacious and very pleasant, though now it carried the sour, sweet smell that inevitably accompanied terminal illness. For all his great wealth, in spite of the best medical attention that could be found and the constant loving care that Tom gave him, the multi-millionaire financier would die soon. Fleetingly, in a mood of unaccustomed introspection, Band wondered if Poston had ever been a truly happy man.

Once, a few years ago, Sir Oliver had asked the doctor if he envied him. Band had laughed. 'The only thing I envy you, Sir Oliver,' he had said, 'is that little Corot in the hall at the top of the stairs.'

'Maybe I'll add a codicil to my will,' Poston had said, laughing in turn.

Dick Band remembered the conversation as he and Tom left the old man's room and smiled to himself, but he didn't linger by the picture as he sometimes did. It was late, and he had another call to make. Besides, he had more practical things on his mind.

'Are you sure you don't want me to organize some nurses?' he asked Tom Calindar for the umpteenth time as together they descended the wide curving staircase. 'You're not as young as you were, you know, Tom, and nursing Sir Oliver constantly must be a strain.'

'Quite sure, thank you, Doctor. I may be sixty-six, but I'm as strong as a horse. Always have been.' Tom Calindar was adamant. 'I've looked after Sir Oliver for over forty years, and I'm going to see him through. He don't need anyone else, leave alone strange women fussing around the place.'

'Right, but remember you've only got to say.'

Tom Calindar nodded. He was a short, thick-set man who made nothing of lifting Oliver Poston's wasted frame, and his hair, in spite of his age, was still only slightly grey. He had been Poston's batman during the Second World War, and had remained in Poston's service ever since.

'Anyway, I'm not alone,' Tom went on. 'The Harmans are very dependable. Mrs Harman's a fine cook, and her husband's always available. And we get plenty of help from the village, seeing as how Sir Oliver overpays everyone. No. Thank you again, Doctor, but we can manage very well as we are.'

'Mr Alan's at the lodge?' The so-called lodge, built near the end of the drive at the same time as the nineteenth-century manor house itself, had been extended by a previous owner of the small Cotswold estate, and was now used by Alan Poston as an extremely comfortable country cottage.

'Yes. He and his friends came down for a weekend party. They often do, as you know.' There was a bitterness in Tom Calindar's voice he didn't bother to hide. 'We've not seen him yet this time. He'll be along when it suits him.'

Dr Band hesitated. It was not strictly his business, but in the ten years since Oliver Poston had bought the property near Colombury and become his patient, he had grown attached to the old man and, whatever Tom's opinion of him, Alan was Oliver's only son.

Band said, 'Perhaps it might be a good idea to mention to Mr Alan that his father's getting weaker. Or would you like me to have a word with him? I'm pretty sure there's no immediate danger, but I expect Mr Alan would want—'

'If it's necessary I'll call Mr Alan, sir.'

Calindar had neatly closed that subject, Band reflected, and without the least impertinence. Now he opened the front door, and bowed the doctor down the steps. Involuntarily they both paused. It was a warm, summer night, the moon almost full, its light reflected by the grey stone frontage of the house. In the stillness of the countryside sound carried, and from the direction of the lodge and its swimming pool shouts and laughter and the splash of water could clearly be heard.

Dick Band paused, struck by the incongruity of the cheerful noises. Then, 'They seem to be enjoying themselves,' he said.

Tom Calindar grunted. 'They always do,' he replied, and added almost to himself, but just loud enough for the doctor to hear, 'but not a thought for Sir Oliver who pays for it all. Vultures—that's what they are!'

As soon as Dr Band's car had disappeared down the drive in the direction of the lodge, Tom Calindar shut the front door, adjusted the lock and the bolts and put up the chain. The drive curved around the side of the house past a garage block to a door which gave direct access to the kitchen premises, and Tom checked that back door with equal care, as well as all the windows on the ground floor. It was a nightly routine, and it took only a little time. The house itself, though more than adequate and totally renovated, was in reality quite small.

Finally, Tom Calindar reached the glass double doors which led from Sir Oliver's study to the conservatory. There were locks, but no bolts, on these doors, and nor were there bolts on the doors from the conservatory to the grounds. Here, as always, Tom shook his head in disapproval. In his opinion this was the manor's Achilles' heel. If ever they were to have a burglar this was the way he would come.

But Sir Oliver had insisted. With only himself and Tom sleeping in the house, he had wanted the Harmans, who lived in a flat over the garages, to have ready access. Tom had seen the point of this, but what he'd not approved of, though he hadn't brought himself to voice his thoughts, was that Alan Poston should be given keys to the two doors. Mrs Harman, who supervised the cleaning of the lodge, had reported that Mr Alan's keys were kept hanging on a hook in a downstairs cloakroom. Anyone—any casual weekend visitor, for instance—could take them and make copies. Tom, thinking of the valuables in the manor, had shivered, and had gone so far as to suggest an alarm system of some kind, but they were much too distant from Colombury for direct connection to the police station there to be sensible; by the time the police responded, thieves could have come and gone. In the end, Tom had acquiesced, and so far there had been no hint of trouble.

His checks nearly complete, Tom went along to the staff sitting-room off the kitchen, unlocking the door to the cellar on his way and glancing down the steep stone steps to make sure the lights were out. Then, reaching the sitting-room, he poured himself a whisky from his special bottle of malt, as he did every night, and sat in the rocking-chair to enjoy it. He had never been a hard drinking man. An occasional beer, a little wine sometimes, and his regular nightcap: that was all he ever took. Idly he wondered if he would be able to afford it in the future.

But Sir Oliver had been generous, even over-generous, he thought. The old man had spent a lifetime in the City, and had turned a fair inheritance into a great fortune, far more than he could ever need, but he had remained the most considerate of men, especially towards those he felt to be close to him.

Several years ago he had bought Tom an attractive small cottage in the nearby village of Fairfield. Beth, Tom's widowed sister, was now living in it, and Tom would undoubtedly join her when the old man died. What was more, Sir Oliver had made provision for a more than adequate annuity payable until Tom and his sister were both gone. With this, his pension, and what he'd saved from an excellent salary and the occasional gift, Tom reckoned he'd not be rich, but he'd still be able to buy his whisky.

Sadly remembering the circumstances that would make this possible, Tom went slowly into the kitchen, rinsed his glass at the sink and left it on the draining-board for Mrs Harman to put in the dishwasher in the morning. Then he turned out the lights and went upstairs. These days he slept in a room along the corridor from Sir Oliver's suite. An electric bell had been installed so that he could be summoned at a touch, but in fact this rarely happened. With the aid of his drugs, Sir Oliver usually slept the night through.

As was his habit, Tom went first to Sir Oliver's room. A dim electric nightlight on the bedside table showed the old man lying on his back. He was snoring gently, each breath so shallow that the bedclothes scarcely moved. But he seemed peaceful and for a moment or two Tom stood looking down at him with affection. Then he straightened the pillows, glanced round to assure himself that everything was in its accustomed place, that the groping hand of his employer could find whatever he needed, and quietly withdrew.

In his own room he undressed and prepared for bed. When he was ready he went to the window, drew the curtains and stared towards the lodge. To judge from the lights shining through the trees and from the noise, the party was still in full swing. Tom Calindar was thankful that Sir Oliver's suite faced the other way, looking across lawns and flowerbeds to the distant Cotswold hills. At least the old man wouldn't be disturbed by his son's incongruous activities.

CHAPTER 2

The party at the lodge that irritated Tom Calindar so much was being held to celebrate Alan Poston's birthday, and the fact that Alan was forty had been the basis of much ribald laughter in the course of the evening. But the laughter was a little unfair. Alan was tall and dark and even though the years of dissipation were beginning to show on his florid jovial face and he needed to watch his waistline, he remained attractive; his dark curly hair and his unusually thick, upswept eyebrows were enough to attract many women. He had inherited a little money from his mother, but it was the allowance from his father that was vital, that allowed him to boast that never in his life had he done a day's work for gain. He had been married for eight years.

The marriage had been something of a surprise in the

circles in which Alan moved. His girlfriends had been apt to be minor celebrities, film stars or television personalities, or rich girls filling in time before a suitable husband came along. Diana Frint hadn't fitted this pattern at all. She had been—still was—a very pretty girl, especially if one ignored the determined line of her jaw, and she was well-educated and intelligent. She had been an excellent secretary before her marriage, but she had no claims to even minor celebrity or notoriety. Her photograph had never appeared in any of the glossy magazines, and she had no money other than what she earned. Diana Frint had been impatient to remedy these two deficiencies.

The right marriage was the obvious answer. Diana had made a point of taking expensive holidays at the best hotels with her brother Guy and their half-sister, Celia. Guy was a couple of years older than Diana, and had been equally well-educated, though somehow he had failed to find himself a permanent niche, and had drifted from one job—usually selling cars or property—to another. Whatever his current occupation, he always seemed able to take time off when he felt the need; possibly a propensity for skilled gambling made this casual attitude possible. Celia was considerably younger than the others, but all three of them shared dark brown hair and blue eyes, and together they made an extremely pleasant trio.

Their relationships were complex, though they never bothered to analyse them. Diana and Guy were close to each other, and Guy especially was fond of Celia, an engaging child. Diana cared less about the girl, but often found her a useful means of introduction to desirable acquaintances. That was how they had met Alan Poston while ski-ing at Val d'Isère; Celia had been rescued by him from a fall into a snowdrift. Three months later Diana became Mrs Alan Poston.

It would be unfair to say the marriage had been totally unsuccessful. In fact, in many ways Alan and Diana were ideally suited to each other, and it had taken them only a few months to adjust to certain unspoken conventions and reach a mutually acceptable *modus vivendi*. Neither of them wanted children of their own, and though they were prepared to cope with Celia, she was luckily at just the right age to be sent away to boarding-school. Diana and Guy between them chose a well-known and highly-recommended establishment. Once there, after the first few terms, Celia found herself spending more and more of her holidays with schoolfriends, while Diana and Alan—usually accompanied by Guy—were busy or abroad.

In fact, both Diana and Alan were happy with a life of pleasure and amusement: a flat in London, the house in the Cotswolds, exotic vacations. Alan continued to have his affairs and, unless they became too outrageous, Diana raised no objections. She too did as she wished, secure in the knowledge that the easy-going Alan, in spite of occasional outbursts of synthetic rage, would never bestir himself to end by divorce an arrangement so convenient for both of them. She was quite prepared to admit that she had never been in love with her husband; she had married him for his money and what she believed to be his social position.

It was on these very points—money and position—that Diana had suffered severe disappointment. Though by the standards of the Frints—their father had been a schoolmaster—Alan was a rich man, he was almost entirely dependent on what Sir Oliver gave him. And the old man, who was a shrewd judge of character, had taken an instant dislike to Diana. His accustomed generosity had failed when it came to increasing Alan's allowance on his marriage. Money, therefore, was not always as abundant as Diana would have liked, and this unpleasant fact often led to dispute.

As for Alan's supposed social position, it was non-existent, at least in the terms that Diana had expected. True, the fact that he was Sir Oliver Poston's son enabled him to run a large overdraft and kept his creditors at bay, but that was about all. It gave him no automatic entry into 'society'—whatever that was—and no special influence in the areas in which Diana was interested. Not that Alan cared a damn. Unlike his wife, he was no snob. Indeed, he preferred to choose his own friends, usually from among those less blessed by circumstance than himself. He seemed to feel himself at home among those whom Diana called 'hangers-on', but he had no wish to be one himself.

The party tonight was typical, Diana thought as she sat on the edge of the large swimming pool in a black and white bikini, dangling her long legs in the water. A dozen people, casually invited, with no one of any importance, not even anyone that Alan particularly liked. Supper beside the pool, hampers of expensive food brought down from London, unlimited champagne. And Alan had had the nerve to take some little bitch up to a bedroom—quite obviously and with no attempt at concealment. He was off to celebrate his birthday, he had said loudly!

At least the girl had left soon after the two of them had returned to the party. In fact, almost everyone had gone by this hour. Five people were staying in the lodge—Diana herself, Alan, Guy, Celia and a house guest, Tony Dinsley. Celia—seventeen, finished with school and preparing for a year with a French family in Paris—had become thoroughly bored with the antics of her elders and had departed to bed hours ago. The rest were still by the pool, together with Frank Leder. Diana wished that Frank would go too. His own home was only ten miles away, not far from the toy factory he owned. He was a bore, an old schoolfriend of Alan's, and the state of the toy trade was such that he was always trying to borrow money. Thank God his wife, Kathleen, who so obviously disapproved of the Postons, had pleaded a headache and not come this evening. Diana shook her dark hair angrily, and pulled a towel round her shoulders. The evening had been very warm, but it was now beginning to get chilly.

'A penny for them, Di!'

Tony Dinsley had swum up to her and, treading water, was gently stroking her bare thighs. Diana glanced quickly at Alan, who was floating on an air cushion some yards away, one hand making little waves, the other clutching a glass of champagne.

'Careful!' she said.

'No need, my sweet. Alan's as drunk as a coot. I doubt if he'd notice if we had it off together here and now. And what do you care, anyway?'

Diana laughed. 'Later, maybe.'

Tony Dinsley hauled himself out of the water to sit beside Diana, also pulling a towel round his shoulders. He was the antithesis of Alan Poston, fair, slightly built, clever and ambitious. One day he thought he might go into politics, but for the moment he was content to be a don at his old Oxford college. He and Diana had been lovers for almost two years.

'Hi! Help me! Help! Nelson! Nelson!' Alan suddenly bawled, falling sideways off the air cushion, floundering in the water, pretending to drown.

It was a game that Alan played regularly with his dog, to the great enjoyment of both of them, if of no one else. Promptly Nelson, a white terrier with a black patch over one eye, who had been feigning sleep at the edge of the pool, leapt into the water and swam for Alan. There was a great deal of splashing, spluttering, barking, until Alan decided he'd had enough, and hoisted himself and his dog on to the air cushion.

'I wonder you put up with him,' Tony said softly.

'Who? Alan or Nelson?' Diana was amused.

'Both. They're pretty well inseparable anyway.'

'Except when we're abroad. So far Alan hasn't been fool enough to try and beat the quarantine rules.'

At the other end of the pool, Guy and Frank Leder were pulling towelling robes over their swimming trunks. Guy called, 'We're going in now. It's getting cold. What about it?'

'Okay.' Diana agreed at once and let Tony pull her to her feet and put an arm round her waist. 'Come on, Alan. We've all had enough.'

'My party! My birthday! *I* say when it's over.' Alan was beginning to get aggressive. 'And you, Tony—you stop mauling my wife.'

Guy intervened, as he so often did to save his sister from embarrassment or dissension. 'Let's drop it, Alan.' he said resignedly. 'At least till we're indoors and we've changed. We really are getting chilled. Look at poor old Nelson. He's shivering.'

'That's because he's enjoying himself,' Alan said, but he paddled himself and the dog to the side of the pool readily enough.

Nelson scrambled out and immediately shook himself, sending a shower of droplets over Frank Leder. Guy, knowing what would happen, had taken the precaution of standing well back. Nor did he make any effort to help Alan from the pool. He allowed Frank to take Alan's outstretched hand, and watched sardonically as with a great heave Alan pulled Frank into the water. Alan roared with laughter.

'Oh come on, Alan. Stop fooling around.'

Diana's voice was sharp, and the glance Alan returned to her was far from kind. He heaved himself out of the pool, and let Guy and Tony pull Frank out. Frank, taken by surprise and hampered by his absorbent towelling robe, had swallowed quite a lot of water. He coughed and choked until Tony banged him on the back, more violently than was really necessary. They were all more than a little drunk.

Guy said, 'Frank's in no fit state to drive himself home. If the police catch him it'll be goodbye to his licence. We can put him up for the night, can't we?'

'I could sleep on the sofa,' Frank said as he caught his breath. 'At the moment I feel as if I could sleep almost anywhere.'

'Of course.' Diana was polite rather than welcoming.

Alan had begun to wend his way along the paved path that led towards the house. Now he stopped and turned back, swaying on his feet. 'There's a spare bed in Tony's room,' he said. 'You can have that, Frank, old boy. Why not? Then you can keep an eye on friend Tony for me, make sure that when my dear little wife tries to climb in beside him he sends her away.'

'Shut up, Alan!' Guy spoke mildly, but there was an edge to his voice.

'Shut up? Why should I? Why the hell should I?'

'Because you're talking filth!' Diana snapped. 'You're tight, Alan, stinking tight.'

'And you don't know what you're saying,' Tony began angrily. 'How dare you insinuate that Diana and I—'

'Oh, come off it! You know it's true.'

'What about that girl you took upstairs a few hours ago? You think you can do what you like, Alan, but—'

Suddenly tempers had flared. They all spoke at once, arguing, protesting. Even Frank Leder, who wasn't really concerned, joined in. Nelson was barking, excited by the raised voices. Then, as Tony took a step towards Alan, he growled fiercely and bared his teeth.

For some reason the dog's reaction restored Alan's good humour. 'Oh, the hell with it!' he said. 'What do I care? A little bit on the side never hurt anyone.' He turned his back on the others. 'Come on, Nelson. Race you to the house, old son.'

What happened next wasn't clear. Afterwards Diana blamed the dog, but it was quite likely that Alan, more drunk than he realized, would have fallen anyway. However, as they reached the patio beside the house, Nelson dashed between his legs. Alan stumbled, but managed to regain his balance. Then he fell again, knocking over an ornamental urn that stood beside the open french windows, and striking his head on one of the shallow stone steps.

He lay for a moment, then seemed to recover, and raised his hand to his head. It came away with blood on the palm. Then he fell back, very still. Earth and rose geraniums and bits of urn were scattered over and around him. Nelson, failing to understand why the game had ended so abruptly, pushed at his master with his nose and started to bark again.

'Quiet, Nelson! Quiet!' Guy ordered.

He reacted quickly. He reached Alan first and knelt beside him, brushing at the debris. The dog withdrew a little and whimpered. The others clustered round, suddenly sobered.

'Is he all right?'

'Guy, is he badly hurt?'

'Take care!' This from Frank, as Guy gently turned Alan's head. 'I'm not sure we should move him.'

'Well, we can't leave him here in his trunks. Get a dry robe to cover him.'

'Shall I phone a doctor? That chap Band?'

Engrossed with Alan and his injury, they didn't hear the sound of soft footsteps inside the house, and they were startled when a frightened voice unexpectedly interrupted them.

'What is it? What's happened? I heard a ghastly crash. Has someone been hurt?'

Celia Frint stood just inside the french windows, bare-foot, a thin dressing-gown clasped round her slender body. With the same hair and eyes, she could well have been Diana in her teens, but her face, free of make-up and soft with sleep, was appealing rather than pretty.

'What is it?' she demanded again, as no one answered immediately.

'It's okay, sweetie,' Diana said. 'Nothing for you to worry about. Alan's had a fall and knocked himself out for the moment. I'm afraid he was a bit drunk.'

At a gesture from Guy, Diana rose from beside Alan and, blocking Celia's view, stepped into the sitting-room. 'Go back to bed, sweetie,' she said. 'We'll look after him.'

'Are you sure I can't help?' Celia asked.

'Quite sure. Go on back to your room. You're only in the way.' Diana softened the words with a warm smile. 'The men'll carry Alan up to bed. Then we'll see if he needs a doctor. I expect he'll be fine in the morning, except for a hangover.'

'All right.'

Celia went, not altogether reluctantly. She was feeling tired and irritable. They had been making so much stupid noise earlier by the pool that she'd not been able to sleep and, just when she had at last dropped off, there had been this almighty crash.

Upstairs in her room, she sipped some water and went back to bed. She lay awake, waiting for the sounds that would signal Alan's passage. Eventually they came, the creak of the stairs, the grunts of effort—Alan was no light weight—the soft oath as someone bumped against something, the whispered instructions, the opening and shutting of the bedroom door. Listening, Celia pulled the bedclothes round her head in irritation. What with school, and her elders' travels, she really didn't know Alan particularly well, and she found it difficult to feel sorry for him after an accident that was his own drunken fault.

Some time later she thought she heard a car either coming or going. She wondered idly if it could be Dr Band. But she was more than half asleep, and she couldn't be bothered to pay much attention to what was happening.

CHAPTER 3

Celia slept late the next morning. It was almost ten before the sun shining on her face woke her. She went along to the bathroom, showered quickly, pulled on jeans and a shirt and ran a comb through her hair. The house was very quiet.

On her way along the passage she remembered Alan and, on impulse, knocked on the door of the bedroom he shared —some of the time—with Diana. There was no answer. Diana, she assumed, would be already up, but she was surprised that Alan should be about, considering the state he'd been in the previous night. She knocked again, more loudly this time, and simultaneously tried the handle. The door was locked.

Shrugging, she ran down the stairs. It sounded as if someone was being sick in the cloakroom and she wrinkled her nose in disgust. She heard the toilet being flushed, and Frank Leder emerged. He started when he saw her, and seemed about to turn away without a greeting.

'Hi! Lovely morning, isn't it?' Celia said ironically. 'You didn't try to get home last night, then?'

'No,' Leder said shortly.

'Let's hope you can make it this morning. You don't look too good.'

Leder seemed to pull himself together. 'If you must know, I feel like hell—and I wish you wouldn't comment on it.'

'Over-indulgence,' Celia said lightly. She didn't much like Frank Leder and she was enjoying herself. 'Where's everyone?'

'In the kitchen, the last I saw of them. I was trying to eat something when—'

Leder stood aside for Celia to go ahead of him. Little bitch, he thought, putting on this damned cheerful act just to annoy me. But she was right about one thing: he'd managed to get up and dress, but the way he felt it wasn't going to be easy getting himself home. And Kathleen! She'd be mad as hell. She'd already phoned once. He ought to have called her last night, but—Suddenly he shivered. Nausea rose in his throat and, hand over his mouth, he dashed back into the cloakroom.

By this time Celia was opening the kitchen door. She was hungry and she was also curious to see what state the others were in. In fact, she found only Guy and Tony, both still in bathrobes, pale and obviously unshaven, sitting facing each other across the kitchen table before cooling cups of coffee. They looked up without any sign of welcome; it was evident she'd interrupted their conversation.

Celia decided to ignore their manners; after all, they were both undoubtedly suffering from monumental hangovers. 'Good morning!' she said lightly, kissing Guy on the top of his head; she was fond of her half-brother, though by now she'd lost any illusions she might have had about him. Tony she ignored, except for a vague wave. 'And how are you two? Not in such a bad way as Frank?'

Tony said sourly, 'Frank shouldn't have had those brandies on top of everything else.'

Guy gave a sudden laugh. 'He needed them at the time. He was terrified. He thought Alan had killed himself.' Both the men were clearly on edge; these stupid hangovers, thought Celia again. Guy was the first to make an effort to speak pleasantly to her, and he confirmed her judgement. 'Look, sweetie,' he said, 'none of us are in the best of shape this morning. If you want any breakfast you'll have to make it yourself. Otherwise there's just coffee.'

'I need more than that. I'm ravenous. I'll scramble some eggs. Sure you wouldn't like some?' she added mischievously.

The two men made no comment as Celia collected eggs and bread and the other ingredients, and merely continued to sit morosely at the kitchen table, without speaking. Glancing over her shoulder at them, Celia asked casually, 'How *is* Alan, then? And what's happened to Diana?'

'They've gone to London,' Tony said.

Accustomed as she was to the vagaries of Alan's and Diana's existence, Celia was astounded. 'London!' she exclaimed. 'But—but surely Alan wasn't fit? I know Diana said he'd only knocked himself out, but still—London!'

'He *did* knock himself out,' Guy interrupted quickly. 'He

hit his head an awful blow though the actual gash didn't seem very deep. But Di was worried about him. We all were. He came round all right, and we put plaster on the wound, but he refused to let us call Dr Band. He said Band might be the old man's favourite quack, but personally he could do without him. He preferred his own chap in Harley Street. Anyway, Di finally agreed. She phoned London and talked to Alan's doctor, and they drove up to town early this morning. "Early" was the word,' he added. 'They were due to see the quack at eight-thirty.'

There was another silence while Guy looked at Tony, who said suddenly, 'Oh, to hell with it! It was all a lot of nonsense. I agree with Celia. Alan would have been· better off staying in bed. If he's got concussion he ought to be resting, not rushing up to town.'

'Sure,' said Guy casually. 'But I suppose someone's got to X-ray his skull and his wrist, just in case—'

'He hurt his wrist too?' Celia was amused rather than sympathetic.

'Yes—and his leg and his back.' Guy grinned at her a little sheepishly. 'In fact, he made a right mess of himself.'

'What! In that case, I should have thought an ambulance was what he wanted,' Celia said tartly, 'not a long car drive.'

Tony looked at Guy. 'I don't think it's as bad as he pretends,' he said at last. 'He just wants Di's loving care.'

'She *is* his wife,' Guy said mildly.

Tony made no reply and Celia, who had lost interest in Alan's misfortunes, concentrated on scrambling her eggs and making toast. When they were ready she brought her plates to the table. Guy poured her some coffee.

'Why's Di and Alan's door locked?' she asked.

'What?' Guy looked up in apparent surprise.

'The door of Di and Alan's room. Why's it locked?'

'Is it?'

'Yes. I tried it on the way down. I thought I'd look in and see how Alan was.'

Guy shrugged. 'Oh, I guess their room was in a bit of a state when they left, some blood on the pillows—not much, but some—that sort of thing. Maybe Di didn't want Mrs Harman nosing around and wondering what had happened—'

The telephone bell in the hall interrupted him, and Guy pushed back his chair. But the ringing ceased, and a moment later Frank came into the kitchen.

'I answered it. I thought it might be Kathleen again, but it was Mrs Harman,' he said. 'She wants to know if she can bring a couple of girls over in about half an hour to clear up after the party.'

Guy nodded. 'Tell her yes, will you?'

Frank hesitated. Then, 'Okay. After that I'll be off. You'll let me know.'

'About Alan? Sure, but don't worry, Frank. Everything'll be all right.'

Frank Leder gave a weak smile, and hurriedly looked away from Celia's eggs. 'Well, I'm off if that's all right. Goodbye. Say thanks for me to Diana and Alan,' he added.

'Will do. Goodbye.' Guy smothered a yawn.

'Goodbye,' Tony and Celia said together.

Guy said, 'Maybe you and I ought to get ourselves shaved and dressed, Tony.' He stood up and stretched.

Tony got to his feet reluctantly. 'As a matter of fact I was thinking of lying down for a bit,' he said. 'I could do with some sleep.'

'Why not?' Guy said. 'As long as one of us is around in case Di phones. What are you going to do with yourself, Celia?'

'I want to go up to the manor and see how Sir Oliver is and say hello to Tom Calindar. I haven't seen them since we've been here this time.'

'Good idea.' Guy smiled his approval. 'But there's one thing—don't mention Alan's accident, there's a good girl. It'd only worry the old man. Leave it to Di or Alan himself. They'll probably be back this evening.'

★

Left to herself Celia made another piece of toast and poured some more coffee. It was being a rather dull holiday, she thought. Then she remembered: you couldn't really call it a holiday. School was over at last—for good, thank God. A few weeks and she'd be away from all this and off to Paris to stay with that family. The ostensible object was to perfect her French, but with any luck it could be a lot of fun. Meanwhile . . .

She finished her breakfast, and hearing voices—Mrs Harman and the girls from the village—let herself out of the back door. She walked down a path that led into the main drive to the manor, glancing idly around her. It was a beautiful day, blue sky, scudding clouds. There was a garden shed on her right, and she had almost passed it when she heard the sounds—scratching noises, whimpering and a sudden sharp bark.

Celia went to the shed and peered through its dusty window. At once she saw Nelson. The terrier was tied to the leg of an old table. As soon as he heard and saw Celia he became frantic, barking and jumping to the end of the bit of old rope fastened through his collar. For a moment Celia stared at him in amazement. Then she dashed for the door. It was locked.

'It's okay, Nelson! Okay, boy! I'll be back!'

She ran for the lodge, barged through the kitchen ignoring Mrs Harman, and hurried upstairs, shouting for Guy. There was no answer, but she could hear the shower cascading in the bathroom and she hammered on the door.

'What the hell's the matter?' Guy, a towel about his waist, poked his head round the door. 'What is it, Celia?'

'Nelson! Someone's tied him up in the garden shed and taken the key.'

'Oh God! Is that all?'

'All? The poor dog looks as if he's been there for hours. He's terribly upset. He's probably got no water and—' Celia stopped, alerted by something in Guy's expression. 'You know!' she cried. 'You shut him up yourself! Why?'

'Oh, for God's sake stop making such a fuss, Celia.'

Celia spun round. She'd not heard Tony come out of his bedroom. She glared at him. 'And I suppose you helped Guy catch him. Two grown men against one poor little dog!'

'Yes. The poor little dog as you call him was whining and crying and making a damned nuisance of himself. It was the only thing to do with him.'

'He was missing Alan, that's all. You know what he's like. He always hates it when Alan leaves him.' Celia frowned. 'I suppose there was no way they could take him this morning. After all, they were only going to London.'

'Celia, we've told you Alan was in a pretty bad state. He was in no condition to cope with Nelson, and Di had enough on her hands with Alan and driving.' Guy spoke with heavy patience.

Celia frowned again. 'Then why didn't one of you go with them?' she asked immediately.

'Because Alan refused to let us. Any more questions?' Tony asked sarcastically.

'Yes. Where's the key of the shed?' Celia demanded. 'I'm going to let Nelson out. He can't be shut up there all day.'

'I don't see why not, if we give him some water and keep an eye on him. But if that's what you want and you'll be responsible for him—' Guy smiled. 'Why don't you find his lead and take him up to the manor?'

'All right. But where's the shed key?'

'Hanging up in the downstairs cloakroom, I think. Now, for heaven's sake, Celia, Tony wants to sleep and I want to finish my shower. Leave us in peace.'

Still indignant, Celia didn't bother to reply. She collected the key and Nelson's lead and returned to the shed with a bowl of water. Usually Nelson was a one-man's dog who merely tolerated others, but now he gave Celia a rapturous reception, alternately lapping water and jumping up at her.

Finally satisfied, he barked to be let out of the shed.

Celia attached his lead and was glad she had for, once outside, the dog immediately started pulling in the direction of the lodge. It took some effort to force him to go with her along the path and on to the drive. But in sight of the main house he was better behaved, eager to arrive, as if he felt that this was where he might find Alan.

Whenever she was staying at the lodge Celia made a point of visiting the manor, where she was always welcome. Now she happily ran with the dog, round the back of the house to the kitchen door. She found Tom Calindar making a pot of tea for himself, and Harman busy cleaning silver. Tom greeted her with pleasure, for he knew that Sir Oliver liked her occasional visits. He offered her tea which Celia refused, but she was happy to share one of Mrs Harman's buttered scones with Nelson.

'How is Sir Oliver?' Celia asked. 'Do you think he'll be well enough to see me?'

'I imagine so, Miss Celia. He had a surprisingly good night. I'll go up and make sure in a minute or two.' He paused, and then added, 'Can we expect Mr Alan to be along later?'

'Alan?' Celia, who should have foreseen the question, was a little nonplussed. She had promised to say nothing to Sir Oliver about Alan's accident, but surely Tom and the Harmans were different. 'I don't know,' she said at last. 'Actually he's gone to London for the day. He had a fall on the patio last night and cracked his head. Diana's taken him to see their doctor.'

The two men exchanged glances. It was quite obvious what they were thinking: Alan Poston had been drunk. But they made no comment in front of Celia.

Celia went on, 'They should be back sometime this evening. It's nothing serious. But I said I wouldn't mention it to Sir Oliver. He'll only worry. Please don't say anything about it, either.'

'As you wish, miss,' Tom said impassively. He finished his tea, swilled the mug and set it on the draining-board. 'I'll go up and ask Sir Oliver if he'd like a visit. Perhaps you'd come with me, Miss Celia, then I shan't have to make two trips.'

'Of course.'

'Better leave Nelson down here,' Harman said. 'I'll look after him.'

Nelson was lying beside the table, looking hopefully for something more to eat. Harman gave him a piece of scone and he made no attempt to follow Celia and Tom. 'Good dog,' Harman said absently as he returned to his silver-cleaning.

Tom Calindar took Celia upstairs. 'Wait here, Miss Celia,' he said when they reached the door of Sir Oliver's suite. 'I'll only be a moment.'

And it was indeed only a moment before, smiling, he ushered Celia into Sir Oliver's bedroom. 'Don't stay too long, miss,' he whispered as she passed him. 'He gets tired very quickly.'

Sir Oliver, however, was having none of this. He had heard Tom mutter something, and had guessed what it was. 'Come in, my dear,' he said, 'and don't pay Tom any attention. I'm feeling very well this morning—very well for me, that is—and I welcome your company. It's good to see someone young.'

Celia bent and kissed the old man's cheek. For all his brave words, she could tell that his health had deteriorated. He was thinner than ever; she felt that if she hugged him tightly he would break. His hair seemed scantier, there were more of those disfiguring liver marks on his skin, and his expression was incredibly weary.

'Come and sit close so that I can see you,' he said. 'My eyes don't get any better. Tell me what's going on in the big world. I want to hear what you've been up to and what you're going to do.'

Celia pulled up a chair and sat beside the bed. Impulsively she took the old man's hand. She told him about her last term at school, about how she'd spent the vacation with a schoolfriend until she came down to the lodge, about the plan for her to stay in Paris for a year from September. After a while she realized that he was no longer listening. His breathing had become regular, though shallow. Smiling, Celia gently released his hand, and very quietly left the room.

She found Tom alone in the kitchen. 'Sir Oliver's asleep,' she said. 'I hope I haven't tired him too much.'

'It doesn't matter if he's sleeping now, Miss Celia,' Tom said. 'He'll have enjoyed your visit.'

'I must be off, then.' She looked around. 'What's happened to Nelson?'

'Nelson?' Tom had forgotten Nelson. 'I don't—' He saw the open kitchen door and stopped. 'Oh dear, I'm afraid Mr Harman must have left the door open and he's run out.'

'Damn!' Celia said.

'I'm sorry, miss, but he can't have gone far,' Tom protested. 'Probably he's run straight back to the lodge.'

'Probably,' Celia said heavily. She couldn't explain to Tom that with Alan away Nelson's popularity rating seemed to be at a low ebb at the lodge. 'I'd better go and find him.'

In fact, Nelson had already been found, and again locked up in the shed, this time with a bowl of water and some food and biscuits. And there he was to remain, Guy said firmly, until Alan returned.

CHAPTER 4

Diana didn't telephone until lunch-time. She and Alan would be back some time that evening. The wound on

Alan's head had needed stitches, though there was no sign of a skull fracture, merely the possibility of slight concussion. But he also had a broken wrist and a strained back. The London doctor had wanted to keep him under observation in a West End clinic for a few days, but the town was hot and stuffy, threatened with thunder, and Alan had refused. He said that if he'd got to spend time in bed he'd damn well do it in comfort in the country.

It was Guy who took the call, and he reported the news to Tony and Celia when he returned from the phone. The three of them, Tony, Guy and a somewhat bad-tempered Celia were having a picnic beside the pool. The meal had been largely silent and the atmosphere strained, but the phone call seemed to relax the men's tension.

'Absolutely typical,' Tony said at length, clearly feeling that some comment was called for.

'Typical? That Alan should insist on doing what he wants? Yes.' Guy agreed. 'But it's encouraging—he can't be in too bad form in spite of all his woes.'

'He won't be allowed any alcohol if there's the slightest hint of concussion,' Celia said.

'No need to sound so pleased about it.' Guy was abrupt. 'Anyway, knowing Alan, I doubt if medical advice'll stop him.'

Tony was looking at his watch. 'If they're not coming back till later I think I'll drive into Oxford this afternoon. There's a book I meant to bring with me and forgot. What about you keeping me company, Celia?'

'Me?' Celia was surprised by the invitation. She always enjoyed a trip to Oxford, and she'd visited Tony's college only once before, and then with Diana. 'Why, yes. I'd like that.'

'Fine. We'll leave in about twenty minutes. Better get ready.' When she had gone into the house he said rather tentatively to Guy. 'You're sure? It's okay with you? You don't mind?'

'Mind? My dear chap, it's a splendid idea, as I said when we agreed on it. Bright of you to think of it. Celia'll be happy, and I'll have the whole afternoon to myself.' He laughed. 'Whatever you do, don't hurry back.'

'I shan't. After all, it won't matter if Di and Alan appear before we do.'

'No. Di said they wouldn't be late, but I'm sure in the circumstances she won't hold it against you if you're not here when they arrive.'

They exchanged amused, if slightly sour, glances. Tony went to collect his car, and Guy carried the remains of the picnic back to the house. The two men had always got on well together though Guy, who regarded himself as a practical man, had tended to consider Tony an intellectual. Now he was revising his opinion. Tony Dinsley, he thought, could show considerable resource when the occasion offered.

And Tony, when the occasion offered, could also be extremely charming, as Celia was beginning to discover. Thus far, she had never understood what Diana saw in him, but this afternoon he was obviously laying himself out to please. He seemed a little *distrait*, and there were pauses in his flow of conversation while he stared silently at the road ahead, but in the main he chatted easily to Celia as they drove, consulting her about plans for the afternoon, implying that she meant quite as much to him as Diana ever had.

'I'd like to leave the car at a garage in St Aldate's,' he said. 'There's something wrong with the timing, and I hope they can adjust it. It's only a small job. After that, Celia, the afternoon's yours. I thought we might go for a walk in Christ Church Meadows, then back to my college for tea. But it's up to you. If there's anything else you'd rather do—'

'No, no. That sounds just great,' Celia said at once.

'Good. Then that's what we'll do.'

The afternoon passed quickly. Tony had clearly shaken off the effects of the previous night, and was good company. Celia found herself interested in the university, listening eagerly as he talked of life up at Oxford, tutorials and lectures, senior and junior common rooms, dining in hall, the great variety of societies, degrees, Eights week, Commem Balls.

'You'd enjoy it here,' he said finally. 'I know you're spending a year in Europe, but after that, Celia—why not? You might need some coaching, but your languages are good. You should be able to get in.'

This was a new idea to Celia, and one she was happy to discuss. A friend of Tony's dropped in after tea, and there was more talk and an early glass of sherry. It was a quarter to six when they reached the garage. Tony went into the office and came out with a long face.

'I should have phoned,' he said. 'The damned thing's not ready. There was more wrong than we thought. The chap says they'll work late on it, but it'll take at least a couple of hours more. I'm sorry, Celia, but we're stuck here at the moment. I think we'd better go along to the Randolph and have another drink and some dinner. We can phone the lodge to tell them we'll be late. They won't worry. How does that appeal?'

'It sounds fine, but—'

'I know, sweetie.' Tony patted Celia on the shoulder. 'It's a pity we won't be there to welcome the wounded hero, but it can't be helped. I'm sure they'll forgive us.'

In the event, Alan was already in bed by the time they got back to the lodge. Diana and Guy were sitting on the patio, sipping long gin drinks and apparently in earnest conversation. Diana looked tired, with dark circles under her eyes, and Guy seemed equally exhausted; one of his hands was bandaged.

'How's Alan?' Tony said at once.

'Asleep and not to be disturbed.' Diana was firm, but she gave Tony a bright smile. 'All's well, or as well as it can be. But of course all this is going to change our plans. Guy and I were just discussing—'

'What plans?' Celia demanded.

There was a pause, and Diana said, 'Our plans for the remainder of the summer, naturally. It was nothing really definite, but Alan had suggested taking a trip somewhere —a cruise, perhaps. Anyway, it's off now.'

'You never mentioned it before,' Celia said.

'Sweetie, does it matter?' Guy intervened. 'Alan's hurt himself quite badly. It's not that serious, but he's got to rest for a while.'

'So it's going to be Dullsville around here,' Tony said, the way he regarded Diana giving the lie to his words. 'It's a shame, but it can't be helped, I suppose.'

'At least Nelson'll be happy.' Celia gave Guy a quick glance. 'He's not still in the shed? You've let him out?'

'Of course. Don't be silly. The first thing Alan said when he got here was, "Where's Nelson?" and he and the wretched dog had an hysterical reunion.'

'He's with Alan now, then?'

'Where else would he be?' Guy shook his head in irritation. 'Really, Celia, you do go on!'

Celia shrugged and there was silence. Tony looked at his watch, Diana stifled a yawn and Guy stretched himself ostentatiously. It was obvious to Celia that she wasn't wanted. Quite clearly they'd all be glad if she went and left them to themselves.

'You've been in the wars too,' she said to Guy abruptly. 'What have you done to your hand?'

'Burnt it,' he said. 'Both of them actually, but this one's rather bad. Horrid blisters. I put them down on top of the stove. You never know whether those damned ceramic hobs are hot or not. Stupid of me.'

There was another silence. Diana had shut her eyes and

seemed to be half asleep. At last Celia decided to take the hint. She said good night and left them. Lingering in the sitting-room as she went, she clearly heard Tony's voice from the patio. 'Celia and her questions! She's becoming a bloody menace! She's worse than Nelson. We need to get rid of both of them.'

As Celia passed the Postons' bedroom door on her way down to breakfast the next morning she heard whining and scratching noises on the other side. They were soft and somehow piteous, and they made her angry. Nelson being a nuisance again, she thought with asperity—just like me. Very carefully she turned the handle of the door and pushed. Today it wasn't locked. She opened it enough for the terrier to wriggle out of the room, and herself looked in.

Alan lay on his back in one of the twin beds. His head was bandaged, but he appeared comic rather than pathetic. There was an empty glass on the bedside table, with the remains of a half-bottle of whisky. The other bed was unoccupied and tidily made up. Either Diana had slept in the adjoining dressing-room or, more likely, Celia thought cynically, with Tony Dinsley.

Quietly closing the door, Celia followed Nelson downstairs. She found him in the kitchen, busily lapping water from his bowl. When it was empty she refilled it, and he continued to drink. He was clearly very thirsty, and his nose was warm. He went to lie beside the back door, but he didn't give his usual barks, asking to be let out. Celia regarded him doubtfully. She was the first down, and there was no one about to ask. Finally, she opened the door and let Nelson out into the garden.

Water for coffee. Toast in the machine. Celia decided against eggs that morning. She poured herself a large glass of orange juice and sat at the kitchen table. She was totally unprepared for what happened next. Without warning, footsteps came pounding down the stairs and first Tony, then

Guy, dashed through the kitchen and out of the back door. It was like a French farce. Diana came next, and she was pale beneath her tan.

The atmosphere changed abruptly. 'You bloody little fool!' Diana said viciously and immediately. 'Why did you let the damned dog out?'

Celia stared at her half-sister in astonishment. She had rarely seen Diana so angry. She opened her mouth to protest, but before she could speak there was an agonized shout from the garden. The two women ran.

The scene that met their eyes was both ludicrous and incredible. On the compost heap behind the garden shed, Nelson stood at bay. Head lowered, teeth bared, eyes bloodshot, he was confronting Guy and Tony. It was obvious that the dog had been digging violently; compost was scattered everywhere.

Guy, wearing only the blue and white striped trousers of his pyjamas, was approaching the terrier slowly and warily. 'Good dog, Nelson. Good Nelson. Good boy,' he was saying over and over, but with little conviction. Nelson held his ground, growling deep in his throat. Suddenly he barked, and Guy backed hurriedly.

The reason for Guy's caution wasn't far to seek. Tony was standing to one side. Regardless of the fact that his robe had come open and beneath it he was naked, he had pushed up his sleeve and was regarding his arm with some horror. Bleeding and bruised, his forearm was already beginning to swell. Nelson's attack had been ferocious.

'The damned dog flew at me and bit me. I hadn't even touched him,' he said as Diana and Celia came up. White-faced, he looked as if he were about to faint. 'He's gone crazy.'

'Oh Christ! My poor darling!' Diana put her arms around Tony and hugged him, taking the opportunity to fasten his robe. 'Guy, be careful!' she cried to her brother. 'Nelson's given Tony a dreadful bite. Don't go near him.'

'What do you suggest, then?' Guy demanded. 'Let him dig to his heart's content?'

Brother and sister faced each other angrily, Diana still beside Tony as if defending him from another assault. 'No, of course not,' she said weakly, 'but surely there's something we—'

'If I had a gun I'd shoot the animal,' Tony said. His original shock was over, and he was furious.

'I'll get a spade,' Guy said. 'A good clout and—'

'No! No! Poor Nelson! It's not his fault.' Celia was vehement. 'He's sick and you've scared him. If you all go away I'll get him and take him to Alan.'

Diana was suddenly very calm. 'Not to Alan, Celia, no. As you say, Nelson may be sick. Let's hope it's not serious, but we can't have him in Alan's room. If he'll let you, you must shut him up in the shed. Then we'll get the vet.'

'All right.' Celia gave in. 'I'll fetch some meat. There's some cold beef in the fridge. That should tempt him.'

Celia ran to the kitchen while the others waited uneasily. They had withdrawn from Nelson's sight, but they could still hear him digging and see the occasional bit of compost flying through the air.

'Bloody dog!' Tony said. 'My arm hurts like hell. What are we going to do with him? Do you think Celia—'

'Perhaps. She's better with him than anyone—except Alan, of course.' Guy laughed.

'It's not funny,' Diana said bitterly. 'The dog's gone berserk.'

'You shouldn't have given him those pills last night.'

'I had to calm him down. He was so excited, hopping on to the bed and off again. Alan—Alan had to get some sleep. Anyway, I don't see what the pills could have to do with it; they were supposed to be sedatives.'

'Here's Celia,' Tony said. 'And I suggest someone comes and helps me cope with this arm of mine before it turns septic. I think it needs a doctor, and I reckon I've done my best as far as Alan's dog's concerned. If Celia can't cope, let's hope Guy can—with a spade if he has to.'

It took Celia five or six minutes to tempt Nelson from the compost heap. Neither Guy nor the spade were needed. The girl was patient and soothing, throwing the dog pieces of meat and bringing him nearer to her with each piece. At last Nelson stood beside her, eating from his bowl, while she stroked him and spoke gently to him.

He didn't object when, the meat finished, she picked him up and carried him to the shed. She tossed him in and quickly shut the door. She felt guilty as he began to whine, but there was nothing she could do. She went back to the house.

Diana was on the phone. 'Yes, a very nasty bite, Dr. Band. No, there's no reason at all to think Nelson's rabid, but one never knows. We've shut him up for the moment and we'll get advice tomorrow. I doubt if the vet'll come on a Sunday.' She laughed. 'Yes, I know, Doctor, but people are different, aren't they? And my house guest—Yes. Thank you very much. Mr Dinsley will be along as soon as he can.'

Diana put down the receiver and turned on Celia. 'This is all your fault,' she snapped. 'If you'd not let Nelson into the garden, none of this would have happened. Do you realize that Alan heard the commotion and came out of his room and nearly fell down the stairs? For heaven's sake, Celia, you're not a child any more. Why do you have to act so irresponsibly?'

'I haven't. Nelson was—'

But Diana was in no mood to listen. 'Our London doctor said it was essential Alan should have absolute rest, and rest he shall have. Guy's taking you back to London today, instead of waiting till September. I'll arrange for you to go to France as soon as possible. You'll have much more fun there anyway.'

'All right, if you want to get rid of me.'

'I'm getting rid of everyone—you and Guy and Tony. Alan and I are going to stay here alone and quietly till he's well again. Do you understand?'

Celia shrugged. 'Okay,' she said. 'And since when have you cared so much about Alan?' she added, but under her breath.

CHAPTER 5

Diana kept her word. She and Alan stayed quietly at the lodge. They had no visitors, except for the vet, Basil Kale, who came and took Nelson away, and Mrs Harman, who delivered food and did a little cleaning. Mostly Alan remained in bed. Diana cooked for him and looked after him, and was generally the devoted wife.

In the middle of the second week of this new régime she went up to the manor. She let herself in through the conservatory and appeared unexpectedly in the servants' quarters. Tom Calindar and the Harmans were having their mid-morning tea in the kitchen. They were surprised and a little nonplussed. If it had been Celia they would at once have asked her to join them, but there was no question of showing such amiability to Mrs Poston.

'Good morning,' Diana said brightly, as they rose to their feet. 'I'm hoping to see Sir Oliver. How is he today?'

'Much the same as usual, Mrs Poston,' Calindar said. 'He's weak but cheerful, and Dr Band makes sure he doesn't have too much pain.'

'Good. Go up and tell him I'm here, will you?' Diana knew better than to arrive unannounced in Sir Oliver's bedroom, even if Calindar would have permitted it. 'Incidentally,' she asked as Tom made for the door, 'has he been told about Mr Alan's accident yet?'

'No, Mrs Poston. We understood—'

Diana nodded her satisfaction. She gave the Harmans a brief smile. 'Fine. You two get on with your elevenses, and I'll follow Tom.'

She left the kitchen, and the Harmans exchanged glances. They said nothing aloud, though Mrs Harman's mouth turned down at the edges. Neither of them had much time for Diana Poston. Alan, in spite of his sometimes extravagant behaviour, and young Celia—yes. But Mrs Poston they found hard to take; in particular they disapproved of her 'fancy man', Tony Dinsley; though the Harmans had only been at the manor for eighteen months, and had seen little of the occupants of the lodge, there wasn't much that had escaped their notice, especially after they had exchanged gossip with Tom. If Diana had known how much they knew about life at the lodge, she would have been very much annoyed.

As it was, she was inclined to ignore the Harmans. Tom —by now a friend of Sir Oliver's rather than a servant— was a different matter, and when he came down the stairs to the hall where she was waiting, she put herself out to be pleasant to him.

'I never asked how you were yourself, Tom,' she said before he could speak. 'It must be a lot of extra work for you, with Sir Oliver so ill.'

'I'm always happy to care for Sir Oliver, Mrs Poston,' Calindar said stolidly. 'I consider it a privilege after all these years. And fortunately I remain very fit.'

'Yes, that is a good thing.'

It was a meaningless remark, and Calindar made no direct reply. Instead he said, 'If you'll come up now, Mrs Poston, Sir Oliver will be pleased to receive you.'

'Thank you.' Diana obediently followed him up the stairs, continuing to make conversation. 'And how's your sister, Tom?'

'Reasonably well, Mrs Poston, thank you.'

'It must be nice for you, having her so close now. I suppose you often visit her.'

'As often as I can, Mrs Poston.' Thinking of Beth, Tom's mood softened involuntarily. 'Actually I'm going over to see her this afternoon. It's her birthday.'

'Really? Give her my best wishes.' Diana sounded positively benevolent.

'I will, Mrs Poston.' Calindar knocked on the door of Sir Oliver's bedroom and, as the old man told them to enter, stood aside for Diana to pass. 'Please don't tire him too much, Mrs Poston,' he said as he shut the door behind her.

Diana went and stood beside the bed. She bent and kissed Sir Oliver on the cheek; it was a convention they both suffered. 'How are you, Father?'

'Not too bad, Diana, thank you. I don't get any better, but my good doctor says anything's possible, and I may surprise you all and live to be a hundred. Wouldn't that be something?'

Diana ignored the malice behind the words, noting yet again the Postons' family voice. In spite of his age, Sir Oliver sounded almost exactly like Alan; on the phone they were indistinguishable. She pulled up a chair and sat down. 'It certainly would,' she said heartily. 'Anyway, I'm glad you're in fair shape, because I've some rather unhappy news.'

'Unhappy news? What? Is it Alan?' The old man was shaken. He gripped the sheet between his fists and made as if to pull himself up. 'Tell me, Diana! What is it?'

'Father, Father, don't get upset,' said Diana quickly. 'It *is* Alan, but he's all right. In fact, I'm hoping to bring him to visit you this afternoon.'

'Ah!' Sir Oliver relaxed. Then he realized the implication of what Diana had said. '*Bring* him? You're bringing him? What do you mean? Why does he have to be brought?'

'That's the point, Father. He had an accident on his birthday, a bad fall. He's got a broken wrist and a strained back. But most importantly he took an awful blow on the head. It needed stitches and he's had to rest in bed for the past few days because of the possibility of concussion. That's why he's not been up to see you before.'

Sir Oliver grunted. 'Dick Band never mentioned it.'

'Dr Band hasn't seen him. Alan preferred to go to his own doctor in London.'

Sir Oliver grunted again. 'How did it happen?' he said.

Diana gave an expurgated account of the incident, putting the blame on Nelson. It seemed to her that Sir Oliver wasn't listening with any interest and she guessed that, knowing his son, he was assuming that Alan had been drunk.

'But Alan's all right now? He's in no danger?' he said as she finished her recital.

'He's a lot better, Father, but not exactly all right,' Diana corrected the old man hurriedly. 'The main thing is his appearance. He looks rather dreadful, which is why I came to warn you. He wants to come and see you, but his head's bandaged, and he looks a bit as if he's been in a war. Really he had quite a lucky escape. The doctor said he could easily have fractured his skull if he'd fallen a bit harder.'

'Well, that's something to be thankful for, I suppose.' Sir Oliver had begun to sound weary, and Diana got to her feet. She had no wish to exhaust the old man so that Tom would have an excuse for postponing the afternoon visit. Once more, in accordance with custom, she bent and kissed her father-in-law.

'Goodbye for now,' she said. 'Alan and I will be along about three, when you've had your after-lunch nap.'

'Right. I'll expect you both. Goodbye, Diana.'

Diana waved her hand and left the suite. In the corridor outside she found Tom Calindar, and for a moment she wondered if he had been listening at the door. She said shortly, 'I've arranged with Sir Oliver that Mr Alan and I will visit him this afternoon, Tom. But don't worry. If there's anything we need I'm sure the Harmans will take care of it. You enjoy your time with your sister.'

'Thank you, Mrs Poston. You're very kind,' said Tom Calindar evenly. But Diana wouldn't have been flattered by the look he gave her retreating back.

At precisely three o'clock that afternoon Diana helped Alan into the car and drove him up to the main house. Mrs Harman had been on the lookout, and was opening the front door before Alan had laboriously got himself out of his seat. She hurried down the steps to offer her help.

'Hello, Mrs H. Come to assist the wounded hero?' he said with surprising cheerfulness.

'I don't know about a hero, Mr Alan, but you're wounded —that's for sure,' Mrs Harman replied. Though she'd been at the lodge on a number of occasions since the accident, she had not seen the victim, and now she inspected him curiously.

Alan Poston laughed, but Diana was unamused. 'It's all right, thank you, Mrs Harman,' she said as the housekeeper offered Alan an arm. 'We can manage very well if we take it slowly.'

'As you wish, Mrs Poston.' Mrs Harman was affronted. 'Sir Oliver's expecting you, so you can go straight up.'

Diana didn't acknowledge this remark, implying as it did that the Harmans had some control over access to Sir Oliver. She merely left Mrs Harman to shut the front door while she herself steadied Alan as he began to climb the stairs.

'Wretched woman!' she said under her breath. 'Why does she have to fuss so?'

'I expect she means it kindly.'

'Kindly!' Diana snorted. 'Anyway, here we are,' she said as they reached the door of Sir Oliver's suite, 'and so far you've done splendidly. Now to cope with Father.'

In fact, they were at first welcomed by Sir Oliver with more than his usual warmth. Though he'd been warned, the old man was shocked by his son's appearance. He made Alan sit close beside the bed, and peered at him anxiously.

'Are you sure you should be up and about?' he asked. 'From what my bad eyes can see, you look like a sick man.'

'It's only this damned bandage. It makes me look a lot worse than I am.' Alan shrugged. 'Anyway, apart from this visit to you, I've not been out and about at all. Di and I have been living like hermits.'

'Accompanied by a house full of visitors, I suppose,' said the old man, with a return to his usual acerbity.

'No, Father,' Diana intervened. 'It's not been like that at all. We're alone, and we have been since just after the accident. Even my brother's gone back to London, and Celia's already in France, staying with that family. They were kind enough to have her earlier than we originally planned, and she's at their summer home.' Then: 'Surely Tom and the Harmans keep you informed about what's going on? They certainly keep an eye on us,' she added a little acidly.

Sir Oliver made no direct reply. He merely asked, 'And how long are you likely to stay here so quietly? Not too many weeks, I imagine. It's not like you, is it?'

Diana answered the question literally, avoiding its implied criticism. 'Alan will have to go to London next week to see his doctor again,' Diana said. 'After that, if he's well enough, we thought we might go abroad for a while, but we'll have to see, of course.'

Sir Oliver moved restlessly in his bed. He wished Alan had come to see him alone. He'd had enough of Diana for one day: she seemed to him such a brittle, nervous woman. His pillows had slipped a little, and she was insisting on rearranging them. He was feeling tired. His hand moved towards his bell, but he remembered that it was Tom's afternoon off and Mrs Harman would answer it, and he desisted.

He said, 'There's one thing before you go, Alan. It was your birthday last Saturday. Your fortieth. You're getting on. There's an envelope for you on top of the chest of drawers. Your usual cheque.'

'Thanks, Dad.' Alan grinned beneath his bandage. 'I thought you'd forgotten me this year.'

'Why? I never have yet.' Alan's remark had made Sir Oliver querulous. 'If you can't be bothered to come and see me, what do you expect? Did you want Tom to deliver it on a silver platter? Or was I meant to give it to your wife?'

Once again Diana intervened hurriedly. 'Father, I told you. We only arrived here in time for Alan's birthday party, and then there was the accident. This is really the first chance he's had to come up to the house. But Alan appreciates how generous you are. We both do. You've always been terribly good to us.'

As the old man turned away from her, Diana made a gesture and reluctantly Alan leant forward and embraced his father. 'I don't know what we'd do without you, Dad,' he said.

'Nor do I,' said Sir Oliver drily.

A moment or two later, Diana declared that Sir Oliver was growing tired, and Sir Oliver made no attempt to demur. With further thanks for the cheque and promises to repeat the visit, she and Alan took their leave. Sir Oliver sighed with relief. The only visitor he really enjoyed these days, he thought wryly, was Dick Band, his doctor.

Dr Band arrived a the manor just as Diana and Alan were leaving. Alan was already in their car, and Diana was seating herself behind the wheel as Band drew up, but she got out again at once to greet Band effusively.

'Good afternoon, Dr Band. Remember us? I'm Diana Poston, Alan's wife.' She gestured towards her husband. 'It must be ages since we all met.'

'A couple of years at least.' Band returned the greeting. 'But we spoke on the phone last Sunday.'

'When our wretched dog attacked Mr Dinsley? Yes, of

course. We were sorry to bother you, but it was a nasty bite, wasn't it?'

'It certainly needed treatment,' Dick Band said, smiling a little uncertainly. He waited, wondering what Diana Poston wanted. On the few previous occasions they had met she had scarcely done more than acknowledge him. He suspected her sudden friendliness.

'You'll be glad to know it's healing nicely,' Diana continued. 'Tony Dinsley phoned from Oxford to tell us not to worry about it.'

'Good. And your husband? I heard he'd had a fall, and I can see his head's bandaged.' They were standing near the Postons' car, and Alan heard the question through the open window.

'I'm recovering too,' he said. 'But it seems to be a slow job. Head and wrist and back all together are a bit much.'

'I see,' said Dick Band. 'Well, I hope all goes well. If there's—'

'But it's Sir Oliver we're really worried about, Dr Band. How *is* he? He looked awfully frail just now—as if he might drift away at any moment,' Diana said sadly.

'Drift away, Mrs Poston?' Band knew perfectly well what she meant, but he disliked the euphemism.

'Die, Doctor.'

'Ah yes. Well, it's difficult to say in cases like this, but we must always hope. Sir Oliver may live a good long time yet.'

Though that's not what either of you are hoping, I bet, he thought to himself uncharitably as he bade them goodbye. What you're wanting me to tell you is that you'll soon be able to get your hands on the old man's money. Personally, I hope he damn well keeps you waiting.

Part Two

CHAPTER 6

It seemed that Dr Band's wish might indeed come true.
Summer passed, then autumn, and as winter came Sir
Oliver Poston continued to survive. He had his good days
and his bad days. He could hardly be said to enjoy life, but
he stubbornly refused to die. Unable to read or watch
television with any comfort, he spent much of his time
sleeping or half-sleeping, but he listened to the radio regularly and his mind remained active.

He was not positively unhappy. Tom Calindar continued
to look after him well, take care of his physical needs, see
to it that he and his surroundings were always clean and
fresh, bring him tempting food carefully prepared by Mrs
Harman, read the newspapers to him and talk of happenings
outside the sick-room.

Without Tom, Dick Band reflected, Sir Oliver would
probably have died months ago, or at least been forced to
retreat to a clinic or a private hospital, where care, however,
expensive, would be less humane and personal. The old
man had few pleasures, but the daily visits from the doctor
were high among them. There was little Band could do for
his patient professionally, but he came as a friend rather
than a doctor, and Sir Oliver looked forward to his coming
as the high spot of his day. Band, who was also the police
surgeon for the area, always had a fund of harmless if slightly
uncharitable stories that did as much to encourage his
patient as any medicaments he could offer.

There were few other visitors during those months. The

old man had never made lasting friendships and by now he had lost touch with most of his business acquaintances. His London lawyer, James Worth, paid a couple of calls at Sir Oliver's request, and the Rector from St Mary's in Colombury, the Reverend Simon Kent, came in occasionally. But Sir Oliver had never had religious inclinations, and though he treated Kent with every courtesy, he saw no reason to change his views at this late stage in his life.

His only close relation, of course, was Alan, his son, and no one could claim that Alan was devoted, or even considerate. Alan blamed his slow recovery from his accident for the fact that his visits tc the manor were relatively rare, though they were now more frequent than they had been in the past. Certainly the accident seemed to have affected the lifestyle of Alan and his wife. They spent much more time at the lodge, and only went up to London when they had to. True, Alan still drank too much, but on the whole he had become more subdued, readier to stay in one place, somehow more dependent on his wife.

Strangely, Diana reacted well to these changes; the accident had affected her too, apparently. Though she and Tony Dinsley continued to be lovers, she was a far more attentive wife than she had been. And even if her motives were, in the end, mercenary, Alan was the gainer.

Those wild weekends at the lodge were now very much things of the past. There were weekend visitors, but the parties were much quieter affairs. Guy and Tony invariably joined them. Frank Leder came sometimes, without his wife, and a few casual acquaintances might be invited occasionally, but usually only for meals. A lot of liquor might be drunk, and a lot of expensive food consumed, but the parties were kept small, and they never got out of hand. Those involved remembered the débâcle of Alan's fortieth birthday celebration and took good care not to repeat it.

One such weekend was planned for the middle of December. The Postons were already at the lodge. On Friday

afternoon Guy drove down from London and Tony came
from Oxford. Frank Leder was expected later in the day,
and half a dozen people had been invited for Sunday lunch.

On Saturday morning Alan and Diana walked up to the
manor to see Sir Oliver. There had been a sudden cold snap
and they moved briskly. Apart from an elastic bandage to
support his wrist, which still troubled him, Alan Poston
looked much as he had done before the accident. The hair
that had been shaved to clean and stitch the wound had
more or less grown back, and his eyebrows had resumed
their Mephistophelian appearance. But he was more
stooped, Diana noticed, and looked older.

'For God's sake, stand up,' she said irritably as they
approached the house. 'You're not eighty yet.'

'Not like the old man.' Alan's laugh was sardonic, but he
made an attempt to straighten his shoulders. 'He's amazing,
isn't he? Last August he was supposed to be on the point of
death, but he's still very much with us.'

'You're not getting fed up, are you, Alan?'

'Fed up?'

'Yes, fed up. With waiting around for him to die? Waiting
to get hold of the money?'

'Well, yes, my dear Diana, I suppose I am, though I'm
as keen on the loot as you are.' Alan kicked irritably at a
small branch that had blown into the drive. 'If you must
know, it's really these dreadful duty visits I hate most
—kissing the old cheeks, pretending to care, the whole
charade.'

'You don't think I like them either, do you?' Diana
snapped. 'But they're necessary, Alan, unless you want him
to cut you off with the proverbial penny. We've got to keep
him reasonably sweet.'

'I know, Diana, I know.' Alan spoke placatingly. 'Actually, I'm not sure Tom doesn't get me down more than the
old man. Talk about a watchdog! Sometimes I feel him
eyeing me as if he—'

'Oh, nonsense!' Diana had no patience with such imaginings. 'He's taken advantage of the situation here, and who can blame him? He's been in virtual charge of the manor for a long time. Naturally he resents the fact that the son and heir's around more than he used to be. But we can't always visit when he's off duty. It would look very odd.'

'I realize that. But you asked, and I answered. To be honest, I'll be more than glad when the old man's handed in his chips and everything's been regularized, as it were. We've waited long enough.'

Sir Oliver had few illusions about his son, but in a perverse way Alan's visits gave him pleasure. The old man suspected that this was largely because he felt such calls to be his due. That Saturday Alan had come in the morning—albeit with that wife of his, as now seemed to be customary—and Dick Band had been in for three-quarters of an hour during the afternoon. It had been a good day, Sir Oliver decided.

He let Tom Calindar settle him for the night with a feeling of satisfaction. He took his usual drugs, though he was free of pain for the moment, and began to compose himself for sleep. His only care was for Tom himself. Tom had the beginnings of a heavy cold.

'Have your whisky hot tonight, Tom, and put a slice of lemon in it. Make it a double,' he ordered as Tom said good night.

'If you say so, Sir Oliver.'

'I do. If that cold of yours gets much worse the doctor will be banning you from my room in case I catch it. And what would we do then?'

'We'd pay no attention to him, sir,' Tom said and grinned, concealing the fact that he really felt quite unwell and would himself be glad to get to bed. 'Good night again, sir.'

He gave a final glance round the room to make sure that everything was in order, and was pleased to see that the old man's eyes were already closed. He turned off the switch by the door, leaving only the soft glow of the electric night-light on the table beside the bed, and gently shut the door. He would, he thought, take Sir Oliver's advice and have a strong hot toddy. Then, with luck, unless Sir Oliver had cause to ring the bell, he might be able to sleep till morning.

Tom Calindar had his extra-large whisky, went to bed and, after a while, fell into a particularly deep sleep. Sir Oliver, as always, slept reasonably well, if lightly and a little fitfully. It looked as if they both would have undisturbed nights.

But in the small hours of the next morning, a shadow darkened the door of the conservatory. By the thin beam of a pencil torch a key was put in the lock and turned, the door opened and shut. A second key opened the second door— into the house proper—and a figure slipped through.

The figure was wearing dark slacks, a dark sweater, gloves and rubber-soled shoes. With no noise or hesitation it sped up the dim stairs and along the corridor to the door of Sir Oliver's suite. Here, for a second, it paused, as if to draw on some secret source of courage. Then, swiftly, it entered.

Once inside, the figure paused again, back to the door, surprised to find the room lit by the glow of the night-light. It was at this moment that Sir Oliver Poston awoke. The two stared at each other in mutual understanding, knowing themselves for what they were, killer and victim.

The killer acted first and with decision, advancing quickly on the bed, pulling a pillow from under Sir Oliver's head and holding it over his face, firmly but carefully and gently so as to leave no marks. The old man made an effort to struggle, but he was mentally shocked and of course by far the weaker physically. His meagre resistance was slight and easily overcome. It was entirely by chance that a weakly flailing hand touched the nearby bell-push.

The touch was so feeble that the resultant ring hardly woke Tom from his deep sleep. It did disturb him, however, and he started, unsure if the bell had actually rung or if he had dreamt it. On any other occasion he wouldn't have hesitated; he would have gone straight along to Sir Oliver's room to make sure that all was well, but tonight, telling himself that Sir Oliver would ring again if he needed to, Tom stayed in bed. Almost at once he was asleep.

Realizing that Sir Oliver might have succeeded in touching his bell and that help might arrive at any moment, the killer fled after one last glance at the old man's still form. Leaving the house without detection, locking the conservatory doors, the killer drifted silently down the drive, carefully keeping to the grassy edge in the shadow of the trees.

As soon as Tom Calindar entered Sir Oliver's bedroom the next day he knew the old man was dead. He put the tray with the early-morning tea and biscuits on the usual table, pulled back the curtains and hurried over to the bed. His first touch on Sir Oliver's cold skin told him he wasn't mistaken. Before turning out the night-light he stood for a moment looking down at the body. In spite of himself he felt tears prick his eyes. He had, he knew, lost a very good friend.

Automatically he picked up a pillow that had fallen on to the floor, tidied the bedclothes, folded Sir Oliver's hands in an uncharacteristic position on his chest and drew the sheet up over the face. Then, remembering to take the tea-tray with him, he went downstairs again.

The Harmans were still in their flat over the garages, and for this Tom Calindar was grateful. He was glad to be alone. He went directly to the kitchen telephone and dialled Dr Band's number.

'Sir Oliver's gone at last, Doctor,' he said softly and sadly.

'He has? You're quite sure?' There was the faintest tinge of surprise in Band's voice.

'Quite sure, sir.'

'Well, it had to come, Tom. He had a good innings, largely thanks to you.'

'No, don't say that, Doctor, please,' Tom answered quickly. 'I—I blame myself. I thought he rang his bell in the night, and I didn't answer it. It must have been the first time ever I've not gone when he called me, but I've got this heavy cold and—Perhaps you were right, Doctor. I *am* old and tired. I should have agreed to have a night nurse. He —he didn't die that peaceful, you know, Doctor. One of his pillows was on the floor. I hate to think of him trying to get help—suffering without me.'

'Tom! Don't be a fool!' Band spoke firmly, sharply. 'No one could have served Oliver Poston or cared for him better than you, and he knew it. You get Mrs Harman to make you a good strong pot of tea, and I'll be along as soon as I can.'

'Very well, sir. Thank you. But—but what about Mr Alan? He and his friends are at the lodge this weekend, but I doubt if any of them will be up yet.'

Even over the telephone Tom Calindar's reluctance was obvious, and Band said, 'Half an hour won't make any difference, Tom. I'll be at the manor by then, and I'll break the news to them. No point in disturbing them before.' To avoid further discussion he added quickly, 'Goodbye for now,' and put down the receiver. Both he and Tom Calindar knew there would be few tears shed at the lodge.

CHAPTER 7

Slowly surfacing from sleep, Diana Poston became aware that the phone beside her bed was ringing. Tony Dinsley rolled away from her and covered his head with the duvet. Diana stretched out an arm and lifted the receiver.

'Yes,' she said, yawning.

'Di, this is Celia. Why didn't you let me know? It was just chance I saw an English paper yesterday, or I—'

'What on earth are you talking about?' Diana demanded irritably. 'Do you realize what time it is? You wake me up and—'

'It's nine o'clock!' Celia was furious, and in no mood to let her half-sister bully her. 'I tried to get you last night, but there was no answer. And you know perfectly well what I'm talking about.'

'We all went over to Burford for dinner, and it turned into a party.'

'Party! A party! Before you'd even bothered to let me know that Sir Oliver was dead. I had to read his obit in the paper. You mayn't have cared a damn about him, Di, except for his money, but I did.' Celia was vehement. 'He was a dear old man and he was always very kind to me.'

'Which was more than he was to me,' Diana said acidly. But she was now fully awake and aware that Celia had to be placated. 'However, let's not speak ill of the dead, as they say. I was going to write to you, Celia, but—'

'Write to me! Write to me? On one of your picture postcards, I suppose; that's all you ever write.' Celia remained indignant. 'You must be mad. Now, when's the funeral?'

'Tomorrow, but—'

'I'll be there. I'll catch an afternoon flight. I suppose Guy's with you and not in London? It doesn't matter. I'll only have hand luggage and I can easily come down by train. Someone can meet me at Oxford, can't they? I'll phone again when I know the time.'

'Celia!' Diana interrupted the flow of words. 'There's absolutely no need for you to come back to England merely to go to Oliver Poston's funeral. It's quite unnecessary. It's not even as if you were a relation of his.'

'I liked him. He once said I was one of his few friends. And I want to come. I'm going to come.'

'Celia, you're just being obstinate.'

Tony Dinsley sat up in bed abruptly, the duvet sliding down his naked chest. 'For Christ's sake, Di, if she wants to come to the funeral, let her. Why not?'

Diana turned on her lover. 'You should know why not. She's bright and intelligent, and—'

'You can't keep her in France for the next year, or however long it—'

'Diana! Diana! Are you there?'

'Yes, Celia.' Diana turned her attention to the telephone.

'You're not alone. You were talking to someone.'

'Yes—er—Alan's with me, of course,' Diana lied. 'He says if you want to come, then come. Actually Guy is still in London. If you let me know your flight, I'll try to arrange for him to meet you at Heathrow, and you can drive down together this evening. Otherwise we'll fix something from Oxford.'

'Okay. Thanks. See you tonight.'

'Goodbye.' Diana put down the receiver and turned to Tony. She gave him a long stare. 'I hope that wasn't a mistake,' she said. 'Remember, we can't get rid of Celia like Nelson. She's my sister, and Guy and I are fond of her.'

'Of course you are. And so am I. But don't worry. We'll cope.' Tony stretched out an arm and pulled Diana down to kiss him.

It was late when Guy and Celia arrived at the lodge, for Guy had insisted on having a meal before they left the airport. They found Diana and Tony sitting in front of a fire, nightcaps before them.

'Alan said to give you his love,' Diana said to Celia. 'He's afraid he's got the beginnings of a cold so he's gone to bed early.'

'I'm sorry.' Celia smothered a yawn. She was tired and quite uninterested in Alan's health, but she added, 'He's recovered from his accident, though?'

'His wrist still bothers him a lot,' Diana said, 'and sometimes he gets buzzing in his head that makes him behave a bit oddly.'

'You mean more oddly than usual?' Tony laughed.

'Don't be unkind!' Guy was grinning. 'At least he looks more like himself now that most of the hair they shaved off has grown back.' He helped himself to a whisky and soda. 'Do you want a drink, Celia?'

Celia shook her head. 'No, thanks. I think I'll go straight up. What time's the funeral?'

'Eleven,' Diana said. 'Better be ready by ten-thirty. We've got to get to the church. He's being buried at St Mary's, Colombury. It's funny really, considering his views on religion, but evidently that's what he wanted—or so his lawyer says.'

'Bloody lawyer,' Guy muttered into his whisky. 'Who ever heard of waiting till after the funeral to read wills nowadays?'

Diana ignored him. 'Afterwards we go back to the manor for a light snack—and, as Guy says, the reading of the will. All very formal.'

'Alan wanted champagne,' Tony said with a wide smile, 'but Di vetoed it. Too obviously a celebration, she said.'

Celia nodded. She disliked the flippancy that seemed to pervade their attitudes to the occasion. In his way the old man had been good to all of them, or at least they'd benefited from what he'd given Alan. To think only of the greater advantages they expected his death to bring seemed to her churlish, but she wasn't prepared to argue about it. They'd probably merely accuse her of being impractical.

She said good night and was at the door of the sitting-room when she remembered the dog. 'By the way, how's Nelson?' she inquired. 'I did ask when I wrote but none of your postcards mentioned him. I imagine he's okay again by now.'

Celia's words were spoken lightly, and she was startled by the impact the question seemed to have on Diana and the two men. No one answered, and the silence lengthened. She glanced from one to the other of them, puzzled.

Then Guy said, 'Sweetie, we didn't want to tell you by mail. We knew how attached you were to Nelson. But the truth is—he had to be put down.'

'Put down? Nelson!' Celia stared at them in disbelief. 'You can't mean it. Why, for heaven's sake?'

'It was essential,' Diana said quickly. 'He was dangerous. He took to biting people.'

'He did indeed,' said Tony. 'You know how he gave me a hell of a bite. I've still got the scar.'

'Yes, but—that was different. You frightened him. Who else has he bitten?' Celia demanded.

'Oh, the postman and a delivery boy,' Diana said. 'He even flew at Alan once.'

'At Alan?' Celia came back into the sitting-room. 'And Alan agreed he should be put down. Heavens, you say I was attached to Nelson, but Alan was crazy about him. I can't understand Alan being prepared to—'

'Celia! Celia, there was no choice!' Diana was impatient. 'As you say, Alan would never have agreed to it otherwise. Nelson was sick. He had to be destroyed. It was a shame but there was no alternative.'

'I see. Poor little dog.' Abruptly Celia said good night again and left them, pulling the door shut behind her with a small explosive bang. She found it hard to believe all she'd been told. She thought it more likely that Nelson had been put down merely because he'd bitten Tony in a panic, and that Alan, still suffering from the effects of the accident, hadn't been told till later. Either way nothing could be done about it now. Nelson was dead—and so was Sir Oliver. She'd miss them both.

The next day, the day of Oliver Poston's funeral, dawned cold and frosty. The mourners breathed out clouds of vapour as they made their way through the churchyard from the road to St Mary's. Huddled in their dark winter clothes, they walked rapidly, eager to reach such warmth as the old Norman building might offer.

The mourners were a motley collection. There were the men from London, lawyer, accountant, trust company representative, bank manager, one or two fellow-directors from companies with which Sir Oliver had been associated; this group held themselves apart from the rest, as if conscious they were out of their element at a country funeral. There were a few locals: Dr Band, and one or two others with whom Sir Oliver had had business dealings. The staff of the manor was there in force—Mr and Mrs Harman, the gardeners, the women who helped with the cleaning and, of course, Tom Calindar, accompanied by his sister, Beth Horton. The chief mourners—Alan Poston and Diana, Guy and Celia, sat in the front pew. And immediately behind them were Tony Dinsley and Frank Leder with his wife, Kathleen.

The service was short and dignified: readings from the Bible, a few prayers, a couple of hymns raggedly sung, and a brief but surprisingly touching address by the Reverend Simon Kent. Celia cried a little, moved by the simple ceremony and the flowerless coffin in front of the altar.

Tom Calindar was also affected, and he blew his nose several times. His face was white and worried and his sister, sitting beside him, regarded him anxiously. 'Tom, are you all right?' she whispered. Tom didn't answer at once and she repeated the question. 'What is it, Tom? What's the matter?'

'Nothing!' He swallowed hard. 'Just let me be, Beth.'

She asked him again as they walked together to the site of the grave, and he rounded on her. 'For God's sake, Beth, I told you. Nothing's the matter. I was thinking about Sir Oliver. That's all.'

'Yes, of course, dear.' Beth Horton, who was not an insensitive woman, reproached herself. The colour had returned to her brother's cheeks by now, and she dismissed the subject from her thoughts.

By the time they reached the graveside the number of mourners had shrunk appreciably, many slipping away to their cars. Those who remained shivered in the chill wind that blew across the churchyard, and all were glad when the committal service was over, and they could decently make their escape.

Diana had tried to reduce to the minimum the number of those invited to return to the manor after the funeral, but she had not been able entirely to please herself. James Worth, Sir Oliver's lawyer, had pointed out somewhat acidly that certain persons would need to be present in order to attend the reading of the will.

'With an estate of this size one has to observe the formalities—the niceties, if you like,' he had remarked coldly, 'and Sir Oliver left me explicit instructions. As chief executor, it is my duty to follow them to the best of my ability.'

Which means being as bloody-minded as you can, Diana had thought, but she'd made no comment. Instead, she had smiled warmly, exuding all her charm, and replied that of course she would do whatever was appropriate. In the end a couple of dozen people gathered at the manor. Among them was Dr Band.

Dick Band was not happy. He had intended to return to his practice immediately after the funeral, but the lawyer had been insistent. The doctor took the first opportunity to phone his wife and warn her that he would be delayed.

'The old man's probably left me a hundred quid. In appreciation, you know,' he said. 'It does happen occasionally.'

'Maybe it'll be a thousand this time,' she said. 'After all, he was really rich.'

'Maybe,' Band agreed. 'Poor old boy. Funny he should have died when he did. I thought he was doing quite well, considering—'

'You always said it could happen any time, Dick.'

'Yes, but I'd have expected to know when the end was coming. However—'

Band returned to the drawing-room, where sherry and open sandwiches were being served. Thinking he should do his duty, he went across to Alan Poston and offered formal condolences.

'Thanks,' Alan said. 'Of course he was an old man and ill, as you know. Best for him he shouldn't linger on too long.' He waved away a plate that Tom was proffering. 'No, thanks. Can't stand anchovies,' he explained cheerfully.

Diana interrupted them. 'Darling, do go and talk to the parson.' Alan obeyed and, as Tom who had been standing staring into the distance, moved away, she said confidentially to Band, 'You know, Doctor, I'm worried about Tom. He's so vague these days. He really has taken Sir Oliver's death to heart.'

Band smiled politely. He had no intention of discussing Tom Calindar with Diana Poston. He was glad when half an hour later, as he was impatiently eating smoked salmon sandwiches and drinking a second glass of sherry, she summoned them all to the reading of the will.

CHAPTER 8

It was some time since the dining-room at the manor had been used. For months the massive mahogany furniture had been covered in dust-sheets, the carpet vacuumed and the curtains drawn back only occasionally, the windows seldom opened. The room had become airless and musty. It couldn't be called neglected—Mrs Harman was too good a housekeeper to permit that—but it was clearly superfluous to the needs of the household.

At least Sir Oliver Poston's death changed all this for a

day. On being told that the will would be read immediately after the funeral, Mrs Harman, who had a fine sense of what was fitting, set to work. Under her supervision, the dining-room was thoroughly cleaned and aired, the dust-sheets removed, the furniture polished. As those concerned with the occasion filed in, the room gleamed; apart from the absence of table settings it looked ready for a banquet.

And a banquet was what some of the potential benefici-aries were expecting, if only metaphorically. James Worth immediately took his seat in the old-fashioned 'carver' at the head of the table, and in spite of Diana's efforts to push Alan to the chair on Worth's right hand the rest of the London contingent of professionals gathered round the chief executor. The family and their associates took places each side of the centre of the table, while the manor staff congre-gated at the far end.

Dick Band, uncertain of his position at the gathering, found himself on the borderline between family and staff—between Celia and Mrs Harman. Tom Calindar was op-posite him, staring dourly into space. The doctor in Band registered that Calindar was looking unwell. Tom was, not unnaturally, taking Sir Oliver's death hard, he thought absently.

He turned to Mrs Harman and smiled. Mrs Harman, taking this as a cue for conversation, murmured, 'Sir Oliver was a good master, Doctor. We've been happy here and we like this part of the country. It's not going to be easy for Harman and me to find a post that'll suit us so well. If you hear of anything, Doctor, we'd be grateful—'

'You won't be staying on at the manor?'

'I doubt if we'll be asked.' Mrs Harman sniffed. 'But even if we were, the answer would be no. I've seen enough of the goings-on at the lodge in the past to know that once Mrs Poston moves in the manor won't be a place Harman or me would want to work in.'

She spoke with some dignity, and Band privately sympathized with her point of view, but he didn't consider it his business to comment. He merely promised to make inquiries and let Mrs Harman know if he heard of any position that might interest her, and she thanked him in a whisper. Mr Worth was calling them all to order, and suddenly the room had become silent.

It was by no means the first time that James Worth had presided on such an occasion. As the silence lengthened he moved his head slowly and looked over the top of his half-spectacles at each of those gathered around the table. Though few of them had heard of him before the last day or two, he knew most of them by name or repute. Oliver Poston had treated him, if not as a close friend, at least as a confidant, and had spoken freely.

'Ladies and gentlemen,' he began, 'formal gatherings such as this are relatively rare nowadays, but certain circumstances and the instructions I have received make this one necessary.' He paused and thought how surprised many of those listening would be if they appreciated the extent to which he could interpret their thoughts.

He went on. 'I have here the last will and testament of Oliver Henry Poston—' As he read, his voice monotonously level, he watched his audience with a certain sardonic amusement. He watched Diana Poston's mouth tighten as he mentioned various large bequests to charities. He saw the genuine pleasure on the faces of Mrs Harman and others who had worked at the manor as it became clear that the old man had not forgotten them; no one seemed disappointed by the relatively small sums. Celia was obviously delighted to be left a thousand pounds as an immediate gift. Only Tom Calindar surprised the chief executor a little. He knew about the very generous arrangements that Sir Oliver had already established for Tom's future, and he'd not expected Tom's totally blank reaction on hearing that he was to receive Sir Oliver's honours and medals, as well as his watch and personal jewellery.

'I come now to the more important personal bequests,' he said, and was amused at the startled expression on the face of Dr Band, who had yet to be mentioned. He continued to read, ' "In addition to the thousand pounds which she is to receive at once I bequeath to Celia Frint the sum of one hundred thousand pounds free of tax on her reaching the age of twenty-one, the said sum to be held in trust until that date. I make this bequest for the express purpose of rendering her financially independent of her half-sister, Diana Poston, and her half-brother, Guy Frint, in the hope that this independence will eliminate or reduce any influence they may wish to exert on her future." '

James Worth paused again. Celia had let her mouth drop open in astonishment, but Diana was white with fury. Alan Poston, however, was grinning. Worth cleared his throat, anticipating the virulent protest that Diana would eventually submit. He wondered how she would take the rest of the will.

' "... a further sum of one hundred thousand pounds, free of tax, to Irene Cassington, my former secretary and mistress, if she can be traced within a year of my death." '

Worth stopped as Alan Poston suddenly began to choke. Red in the face, tears streaming from his eyes, he hawked and spat into his handkerchief. Dr Band started from his place, but someone hurriedly poured water from the cut-glass jugs already on the table. Alan drank gratefully, and his coughing subsided.

'Sorry about that,' he said finally, mopping his face. 'I must have just caught my breath. Silly of me.'

Diana was full of solicitude. 'You're all right now, darling? You're sure?'

'Yes, yes. I'm fine.' Alan was clearly irritated by his wife's attention. 'Let's get on with it. You were saying, Mr Worth —a hundred thou to one of my father's old flames if she can be traced. What if she's dead too?'

'It's a little out of order for the reading to be interrupted in this way, Mr Poston,' Worth said severely, 'but I can tell you that Irene Cassington has already been traced. The matter was put in hand some while ago when Sir Oliver was revising his will. It was not an easy task, as the lady in question had married twice and, of course, her name had changed on each occasion. She had also moved her residence several times. In fact, it was only a few days ago that we established that she's been dead for a number of years.'

'So what happens to the money?' Diana demanded.

'Under the terms of the will, it reverts to the estate, Mrs Poston. Now—' Worth drew a deep breath. He had had enough of the Postons for the moment, and wished to bring matters to a seemly conclusion without further interventions. 'Now we come to Sir Oliver Poston's paintings, and here I will interpret the carefully-drafted legal verbiage, if I may call it that.' He coughed and waited, as if for some answering smile. None came and he went on. 'As most of you will know, Sir Oliver possessed a moderately-sized but valuable collection of paintings. This collection is scattered, and many of the works are at present on loan to various galleries throughout the country. It was Sir Oliver's wish that on his death these loans should become outright gifts. As for the paintings now hanging in this house, which were his favourites, these are to go to the nation with—'

This was too much for Diana Poston. 'Mr Worth,' she interrupted again, 'are you telling us that the manor is to be denuded of all its treasures? Because that's absurd. They're a part of the place and—'

'Mrs Poston, for the moment I have to assume that you and all present are prepared to respect Sir Oliver's last wishes. Even if I am wrong, it makes no difference. I drew up this will myself, and I am as certain as it is possible to be that it is good in law. Any attempt to contest it will be likely to fail. And it will be the duty of the executors to exert their utmost efforts to see that the intentions of the testator are fulfilled.'

Worth paused and regarded his audience for a moment before continuing, 'There is one matter that may as well be made clear immediately, though it is perhaps a little out of sequence. The executors are myself, assisted by—' He named two of the faceless men from London. Sir Oliver had not chosen his son as one of his executors, and the point was not lost on Diana or her husband, Worth noted. Diana glared at Worth, as if the latter were personally responsible for Sir Oliver's judgement. War between the two of them had now been openly declared, Dick Band thought as he watched the chain of action and reaction with detached interest.

But Band in his turn was soon to be disturbed. 'As I said, the paintings in the manor are to be a gift to the nation— we shall of course hope to make arrangements with the Inland Revenue to accept their value as part of the transfer tax that will have to be paid on the estate—with one exception. The exception is a Corot painting, which goes to Dr Richard Band. And here I quote, "Dick Band may not be the world's best-known doctor, but he has shown me real kindness and this is my way of thanking him." I should add that the bequest is accompanied by a sum of money which should yield sufficient income to insure the painting adequately while it is in the doctor's possession.'

Dick Band couldn't believe it. Admittedly Sir Oliver had mentioned the possibility, but that had been in the course of an exchange of banter. Never for one moment had Band dreamt that the painting would some day be his. And he was embarrassed by what had been said of him. He had come to like Oliver Poston, and he'd done his duty as a doctor. That was all.

It was a full minute before he was again concentrating on the speaker, and Worth had almost come to an end. Band caught the words, '. . . residue of my estate . . .', and a few moments later '. . . until the will is probated Mr Calindar and Mr and Mrs Harman will remain in charge of the manor, under the supervision and at the discretion of the executors, and Mr Alan Poston will retain right of abode in the lodge and the flat in London which he uses at present.'

Diana and Alan Poston had been murmuring to each other. Now Alan said, 'This residue of the estate—what's left over when everything's been settled—how much shall I get?'

Worth glanced round the room and finally turned a cold eye on Alan. 'I'm not sure, Mr Poston, that your question is entirely appropriate at this semi-public gathering. In fact, I do not know precisely, but the sum should not be inconsiderable. Taking into account the manor and the other properties, and subject to successful negotiations with the revenue authorities, I would estimate the residue to be in the region of several million pounds sterling.'

There was a murmur around the table, and Alan drew in his breath sharply. He grinned as if in anticipation.

'How long will probate take?' Diana asked abruptly.

Again Worth admitted that he could not say precisely, but would estimate from six to twelve months. Sir Oliver's affairs were in apple-pie order, he assured her, but the settlement of a large estate always took time.

'So that the lawyers can take as much as possible,' Diana said loudly to no one in particular.

James Worth, however, chose to answer. 'That is an uncalled-for remark, Mrs Poston, if I may say so. But nevertheless it may in certain circumstances have some truth in it. Lawyers are only human. Like other humans some tend to suffer from a deadly sickness.'

'What on earth do you mean?' Diana said. 'What deadly sickness?'

'Greed, Mrs Poston,' Worth said. 'Greed.'

The remark was intended as a rebuke to Diana—well justified, Band thought: Worth was showing a surprising bent for repartee. But the doctor himself, in common with most of the others in the room, felt a twinge of conscience.

An exception was Tom Calindar. His mind was totally preoccupied with other matters; the reason why he had shown no reaction to the small but very personal gifts that Sir Oliver had left him was because he had not heard a word that Worth was saying.

Tom Calindar was a very worried man. He had a problem with which he felt completely unable to cope. He needed help, and had no idea where he should seek it. He had no wish to involve his sister, and neither Beth—nor for that matter Mr or Mrs Harman, whom he thought of next—had any authority. He needed someone who would first of all believe him, and secondly be prepared to act on that belief.

Mr Worth was perhaps the obvious person, but the lawyer's dry, acidulated manner had caused Tom to dismiss that idea; he doubted his ability to convince James Worth, especially as he was still only half convinced himself. Tom thought of the parson. At least this was someone who, because of his calling, would listen and respect what he was told. But the Reverend Simon Kent, though clearly a kind man, hardly inspired confidence.

And that, Tom Calindar decided, left Dr Richard Band. He trusted him as a true friend of Sir Oliver's, but he was fearful that the doctor would merely laugh and tell him to take more water with his whisky. Still, Band it would have to be.

His mind made up, Calindar acted at once. He caught Band as the doctor was putting on his coat in the hall of the manor and said, 'Sir, could I have a word with you?'

'Now, Tom? What about? Your health?'

'No, sir. Not my health. It's a—a private matter.'

Tom had not judged his moment well. Diana Poston was immediately behind him, and had overheard his request. He turned in surprise when he heard her voice say, 'And certainly not now. You know there's a lot to be done here, Tom. If it's a private matter I'm afraid it'll have to wait.'

She smiled brightly but determinedly at Band, but the

doctor ignored her and spoke directly to Calindar. 'Would tomorrow be all right, Tom? I've a morning surgery, but if you could come in about twelve—'

'Thank you. Yes. That would be fine, Doctor.'

Calindar returned to his duties with what was almost a sense of relief. His purpose was unchanged. He still had every intention of confiding in the doctor, but at least he didn't have to face the issue today. In any case, the delay was trifling and would give him a chance to marshal his thoughts so that he would be able to explain his worries clearly to Band.

CHAPTER 9

That evening, after the legal and social formalities had been completed for the moment, and all the mourners had departed leaving the manor to Tom Calindar and the Harmans, Celia came out of her bedroom at the lodge just as her brother-in-law, Alan, emerged from his. They met in the passage, and he promptly put out an arm and pulled the girl to him.

'Hi, sweetie,' he said. 'How does it feel to be an heiress? You'll have plenty of boyfriends after you now, you know. As if you haven't had plenty already, I'll be bound.'

'Let me go, Alan.'

Celia, surprised, tried to push him away. His leer was unpleasant and his breath, hot on her face, stank of whisky and revolted her.

'Give us a kiss, Celia.'

'No!' Angrily she turned her head away from him. 'Don't be silly, Alan. Think of Diana.'

'Why the hell should I think of Diana? All she ever thinks of is Tony Dinsley.' Holding her to his side with one arm, Alan was bending his head and still trying to kiss her, while his free hand was fumbling with the buttons on the front of her dress. 'Come on, sweetie. Be kind to me. You've got nothing to lose.'

'Alan! Leave me alone!' Celia had never before known him to act in such a fashion. There had been the occasional hug, the slap on the bottom, the casual kiss, but this type of assault—for it really was taking on the dimensions of a genuine assault—was quite new. 'Leave me alone!' she repeated. 'Or I'll scream. I'm not one of your little whores.'

'No, but I wish you were, sweetie.'

This was too much for Celia, especially as Alan had succeeded in unbuttoning the top of her dress. As she felt his hand slide beneath her bra she twisted her foot and brought the sharp heel of her shoe down on his instep with all the force she could muster.

It was enough. Alan gave a short shout, and a curse. But he released her and she dashed for the bathroom, leaving him to inspect his injured foot. She stood with her back to the locked door, breathing hard. Then after a moment she began to laugh. Poor old Alan! What a ludicrous situation, she thought.

Celia waited for some five minutes and then opened the bathroom door cautiously. There was no sign of Alan, and she went downstairs. Voices were coming from the sitting-room, angry voices, argumentative voices. She thought she heard her own name mentioned, though she wasn't sure. What was certain was that as she came into the room there was a sudden silence.

They were sitting around the fire, clasping pre-dinner drinks. Diana and Tony were close together on the sofa, Alan and Frank Leder in comfortable chairs, Guy cross-legged on the floor. They looked a pleasant, happy group. Beyond a curious stare at Alan, Celia showed no awareness of their recent encounter. Instead she asked after Kathleen, Frank Leder's wife.

'She didn't want to stay,' Diana said, patting the sofa as an invitation to Celia to join her and Tony.

'What will you drink, Celia?' Guy was on his feet.

'Give her champagne,' Alan said. He grinned at Celia, evidently bearing no grudge for his bruised instep. 'And you can fill up my glass at the same time, Guy. This is a celebration!'

'Celebration?' said Celia. 'Why should we celebrate Sir Oliver's death?'

'Why celebrate? Listen to the girl,' Alan said. 'Don't be so naïve, Celia. You know perfectly well we're celebrating all that lovely loot we're going to get, that's why.' He lifted the glass that Guy had refilled and drained it again. 'Let's drink to it one more time. To riches!'

'To riches!' Guy and Tony shouted in unison.

'And prosperity,' Frank added a little pompously.

Diana took no part in the toast. 'You're drunk,' she said. 'All of you. The old man screwed us. Giving away all those paintings! Why, that Corot he left to his wretched doctor must be worth a packet by itself.'

'Come on, Di,' Guy expostulated. 'Don't sound so damned mean. You can afford it. You heard what that old fool Worth said—the residue of the estate's going to come to a very tidy sum indeed, even when the lawyers have finished with it. And remember, once she comes of age, we won't have to support our young sister any more.' He lifted his glass to Celia. 'To our heiress.'

'I'm very grateful to Sir Oliver,' Celia said coldly.

'So are we all,' Alan said with great solemnity. 'So are we all.'

It wasn't a particularly funny remark, though Alan's manner had been slightly satirical. But everyone, even Diana, laughed and Celia wondered why. She felt as if she were being excluded from a family joke, a family of which both Tony Dinsley and Frank Leder had somehow become honorary members.

★

Not many miles from the lodge Dick and Mary Band were entertaining Basil Kale, the vet, and his wife Monica to drinks and a casual supper. The four of them were old friends, and the talk naturally turned to Oliver Poston's funeral.

'Maybe I should have gone,' Basil Kale said, 'but I scarcely knew him, and anyway I had better things to do, like bringing a lovely little foal into the world. A breech birth, but I'm glad to say mother and child are both doing well.'

For a few moments they discussed horses, and Kale suggested amid laughter that Band should sell the Corot Oliver Poston had left him and buy a potential Derby winner. Then the conversation returned to the manor and what might happen to it now.

'Let's hope Alan Poston sells and he and that wife of his clear out of the neighbourhood,' Kale said frankly, 'but I suppose that's too much to hope for.'

'They're not exactly Basil's favourite people, as you know,' his wife said. 'He's never forgiven them for the way they treated Nelson.'

'And I never will,' Kale said firmly. 'At one point Alan Poston's almost beside himself because a car's sent Nelson flying into a ditch—the dog only had a minor cut on his leg —and then a few months later he insists the animal should be put down because he's taken a little nip out of one of his precious friends.'

'More than just a little nip,' Band remarked mildly. 'It was quite a nasty bite, as I remember.'

'Okay, okay! But what had the Postons been doing to the poor brute? I've told you before, Dick—I swear the dog was half-doped and he got scared and that's why he bit that chap. Serve the man right.' Kale, guaranteed to be even-tempered only in the company of animals, was bristling with indignation.

To divert him, Mary Band said, 'And how *is* Nelson? He's settled down in his new home?'

'Splendidly!' Basil Kale's face was suddenly wreathed in a smile. 'Much better than I'd hoped. He pined a bit at first, naturally, but having a young boy to play with has made all the difference. He's fine now.'

Monica Kale smiled too, but wryly. 'Everything seems to have turned out all right, but Basil took an awful risk. The Postons could have made a lot of trouble. After all, Nelson belonged to them and if they wanted him destroyed—'

'I wasn't going to put down a fine healthy animal just to satisfy the Postons' whims,' Kale interrupted. 'If they wanted that they should have gone to another vet.' Suddenly he grinned. 'But I made sure they didn't by agreeing to do the job. Anyway, I never sent them a bill, so they can't get me for that.'

The Harmans had insisted that Tom Calindar should have supper with them that evening. 'It's funny,' Mrs Harman said, 'but the worst time is always after the funeral—that is if you're fond of whoever's died—not after the death. Believe me, I know. I remember when my poor dad went, and my first hubby.'

'It's the let-down; it's kind of an anti-climax,' her present husband said. 'At first there's always so much to do you don't have time to think.'

'Anyway, this is no night to be alone, Tom. You're having supper with us,' Mrs Harman declared.

Calindar hadn't resisted. He got on well with the Harmans, who had never intruded on his privacy, and his mind had been less troubled ever since he'd made a firm arrangement to talk to Dr Band in the morning. He enjoyed the evening—he knew the Harmans' company had stopped him from fruitless brooding—and he stayed later than he had intended.

In fact, it was after midnight when he left the Harmans'

flat over the garages, and it was cold. He walked the few steps
to the main house briskly, his breath fogging the air in front
of him, meaning to let himself in by the conservatory door.
He found it unlocked.

Quietly he entered the conservatory, and very gently tried
the door that led into the house. That, too, was unlocked.
Tom knew that these open doors were not due to any error
on his part. In spite of his preoccupations, he was certain
that he had locked both doors some hours ago when he left
the house. In his absence someone had been inside the
manor; what was more, the intruder might still be there.
Tom thought of returning to the flat and asking Harman to
join him, but he dismissed the idea. It could only be someone
from the lodge, he told himself, since there were no signs
that the doors had been opened other than with keys.

Reproaching himself for his moment of panic Tom Calindar went inside, turning on lights and calling, 'Hello! Who
is it?'

'Hello, Tom. It's me.'

Tom swung round. 'Ah,' he said, 'so it is.' He wasn't
prepared to admit that he'd been alarmed. 'This is a late
visit. Is there something you want?'

'Yes. Champagne. We've run out at the lodge, so I
volunteered to fetch more from here. Two or three bottles
will do. Would you get them for me, please?'

Champagne! On this night! And at this time of night,
Tom, thought, but it didn't occur to him to refuse. He
fetched the key from the kitchen, unlocked the cellar door
and switched on the light at the top of the steep stone steps.

'The Veuve Clicquot, will that do? Three bottles?' he
inquired.

He never heard the reply. A bunched fist hit him between
the shoulder-blades and he was falling, flailing the air with
his arms and legs, his breath sucked out of him as he gasped
with surprise at the attack. He scarcely felt his sudden hard
contact with the cellar floor.

Behind him his assailant moved swiftly, hurrying down the steps to stand by the still figure, bending over, carefully inspecting the damaged skull and the pool of blood, raising one of Tom's eyelids, and holding the back of a hand in front of Tom's nostrils to check for breath.

Satisfied that Tom Calindar showed no signs of life, his assailant took a bottle from a pocket, and carefully keeping out of reach of the splattering alcohol, poured a liberal amount over Tom's face and clothes. A glance to ensure that all was as it should be, a wrinkled nose at the stink of gin, and Tom Calindar was alone.

CHAPTER 10

It was Mrs Harman who found Tom Calindar's body the next morning.

When the Harmans arrived at the manor at their usual time of eight-thirty they were surprised to discover that the back door was still locked. Nor, peering through the kitchen window, could they see any sign of Tom though, now he had no duties to perform for old Sir Oliver, they would have expected him to be lingering over a cup of coffee.

'He's probably overslept,' Harman said. 'I'll nip back to the flat and get the conservatory keys.'

The Harmans let themselves into the house the same way as Tom and his murderer had done the previous night. Mrs Harman went straight to the kitchen and her husband went upstairs, prepared to root Tom out of bed and make a joke of his oversleeping. But he found Tom's room empty and the bed either unslept in, or remade, and this worried him. His first thought was that perhaps Tom had gone to the bathroom and had a fall; bathrooms were places where people did slip. But the bathroom, too, was empty.

Harman quickly looked into Sir Oliver's suite, and made

a quick search of the other rooms on the bedroom floor. He was hesitating about going up to the attics when he heard his wife calling.

She was waiting for him at the bottom of the stairs. Her face was pale, her mouth set, but she was completely in control of herself. Her voice was steady and matter-of-fact.

'I've found Tom,' she said. 'The cellar door was ajar and I noticed the light was on. He's down there. He's dead.'

'Dead! You're sure?'

'Quite sure. I went down. He must have slipped on the top step and fallen all the way by the looks of it.'

'But why—' Harman shrugged as he started towards the cellar. Pointless to ask why Tom Calindar should have decided to go down there after midnight. Perhaps he thought he'd heard something. Perhaps—'Poor devil,' he said.

'Yes. Poor old Tom. He was a good man.'

Harman went down the cellar stairs slowly and carefully. A glance was enough to assure him that his wife had made no mistake; Tom Calindar was undoubtedly dead. He returned to the kitchen and found her making a pot of strong tea.

He took a mug and sipped it gratefully. 'What should we do? Phone the lodge?' he wondered aloud.

'I suppose so,' his wife answered. 'They'll have to know.'

'Fat lot any of them will care.' Harman was bitter. 'No. Dr Band's the chap to phone first. He'll know what the form is, and he'll know how to break it to Tom's sister. It's going to be a blow for her.'

Some thirty minutes later Harman opened the front door of the manor to Dr Band and immediately showed him down to the cellar. All doctors are used to death and Dick Band, as the police surgeon for the district, was not unaccustomed to accidental and violent death. But for a moment he stood looking with pity at Tom Calindar's sprawling body. Then he began his preliminary examination.

The smell of gin had dissipated somewhat during the night, but Dr Band caught it at once as he knelt down. He paused, frowning. As far as he knew, Tom Calindar never drank gin. But he completed his work, and found nothing ususual. The cause of death was obvious—multiple injuries resulting from a fall down a steep flight of stairs to a stone floor. Probably the injury to the head had been the most damaging. He put the time of death between midnight and four in the morning.

Standing up, Band measured with his eye the incline of the stairs and the position of the body. Tom, he thought to himself, had come quite a cropper, probably from the top. Had he been drunk? He was used to the steps and they were well-lighted. And anyway, what was he doing there in the middle of the night? Getting another bottle? If so, who could blame him in the circumstances. But gin?

When he went upstairs, after he had telephoned Sergeant Court at Colombury police station and reported the death as an apparent accident, he didn't hurry away. He refused Mrs Harman's offer of a cup of tea, but settled for instant coffee and sat himself down at the kitchen table as if he had nothing to do for the rest of the day except chat to the Harmans.

'I suppose you'd not seen Tom since yesterday afternoon,' he said conversationally.

'That we had,' Mrs Harman took him up at once. 'As I said to my hubby, the night of a funeral's no time to be left alone, and Tom was really fond of old Sir Oliver. They'd been together a long time, as you know, Doctor. So we insisted he should come and have supper with us.'

'Kind of you,' Band murmured.

'Not a bit.' Mrs Harman brushed his remark aside. 'I'm only too glad Tom enjoyed his last evening, because I'm sure he did. We had a nice meal and a bottle of wine, and

Tom was full of plans for his future with his sister.'

'Yes, his poor sister,' Harman said. 'We're hoping you'll break it to her, Doctor. The wife and I hardly know her and it would come better from you.'

Band reviewed his morning. He had a call to make in another village, but he could drop in on Beth Horton on the way and still not be too late for his morning surgery. The thought of his surgery reminded him that Tom had been going to visit him about noon to talk about 'a private matter'. He wondered if Mrs Horton would know what that might have been.

He said, 'Yes, all right. I'll tell Mrs Horton. Incidentally, I thought when I saw Tom yesterday that he wasn't looking too well. I suppose he didn't have a lot to drink last night, did he?' He grinned to show he wasn't meaning to disapprove.

Harman shook his head. 'If you mean he fell down those stairs because he was drunk, Doctor,' he said bluntly, 'the answer's no. We shared a bottle of wine between three of us, but that was all. We offered him a nightcap before he left—around midnight, that was—but he refused.'

'I know he always had a whisky just before going to bed,' Mrs Harman said, 'but he'd have had that here in the kitchen or in the staff sitting-room.' She glanced over her shoulder at the empty draining-board by the sink. 'That's funny,' she added. 'He always rinsed his glass and left it there to go in the dishwasher the next morning. He can't even have had his whisky last night; there's no glass.'

'I suppose he might have washed it up for once,' Band remarked.

'Perhaps,' admitted Mrs Harman doubtfully. 'But he was very much a man of set ways—routine, you might say. And he always felt glasses and things weren't really clean unless they'd been in the dishwasher.'

Band stood up slowly, considering the position. It was true there seemed to be one or two anomalies attached to Tom's death, but hardly enough to bother the police.

There'd be a PM and an inquest, of course, but the verdict was certain to be accidental death. Even under the stress of losing Sir Oliver—even if he were a little drunk—Tom Calindar would have enough sense not to try to commit suicide by throwing himself down a flight of cellar steps. At least that was a certainty.

Band said, 'Well, if I'm to call on Mrs Horton I'd better be on my way. Sergeant Court will be here and he'll cope with the immediate formalities. Just answer his questions and cooperate with him. And I suggest you telephone Mr Worth and tell him what's happened. You've got his London number?'

'Yes, Doctor.' Harman nodded. 'He told Tom not to hesitate to phone him if there was anything we wanted. I must say, we never thought it would be anything like this.'

'No, I'm sure you didn't.' Band, struggling into his over-coat, smiled from one to the other of them; he thought they were behaving admirably. 'Right then. If there's nothing else, I'll be off.'

The Harmans exchanged glances. It was Mrs Harman who spoke. 'Doctor, who's to inform Mr Alan? He should be told, shouldn't he?'

'Yes, I suppose so,' Band said reluctantly. He'd quite forgotten Alan Poston for the moment, and Diana. Obviously they had to be told, but not by him if he could avoid it. The front doorbell solved the problem. 'That'll be Sergeant Court. I'll have a word with him on the way out. The police can tell the Postons.'

But there was no way of avoiding a call on Beth Horton, and she took the news hard. She didn't cry. She showed no emotion. She was cold, distant, frozen. Dick Band hid his distress as he watched the signs of shock; he'd seen women like this before, and he knew that when she broke she would need support.

'How could it have happened?' she demanded. 'What was

Tom doing going down to the cellar at that time of night?
Was he drunk, Doctor?'

Band was surprised by the direct question, but tried not
to show it. He shrugged. 'Beth, you know your brother was
an abstemious man as a rule, but he'd been under quite a
strain in the last few days, and yes, he had been drinking.
The Harmans served wine with supper, and Tom seems to
have had some gin when he got back to the manor, though
how much I don't know.' He waited for her to comment,
and when she didn't he added, 'Tom didn't usually drink
gin, did he?'

'No. He preferred whisky.' Beth Horton's thoughts were
clearly elsewhere. 'He said whisky never bothered him, but
gin always seemed to have a kick behind it.'

Band almost sighed with relief. At least he had found a
reasonable explanation for Tom's sudden change from his
customary whisky to gin. Depression had hit him, and he'd
wanted to get tight. Then a moment of carelessness at the
top of the cellar stairs—Perhaps he'd been in search of
another bottle. It could have been as simple as that.

He said, 'Tom was coming to see me this morning about
something he called "a private matter". Would you have
any idea what he meant, Beth? He said it wasn't his
health.'

She stared at Band blankly. 'I've no idea. But he did have
a cold and he's certainly not been his old self lately.'

'How do you mean?

'Well, Doctor,' Beth said. 'He's been a bit worried and
irritable—even before Sir Oliver died. And he's been worse
since, of course.' Remembering Tom, Beth was unexpectedly overcome by grief and began to cry unrestrainedly.

Through her tears, she added, 'First Sir Oliver, and now
Tom. I wonder who'll be buried from the manor next.'

CHAPTER 11

Dr Band was very busy during the next few days. Not only was there the usual crop of winter ailments for him to contend with, but an outbreak of hepatitis was threatening to shut the local school and spread through Colombury. When a fellow doctor went down with influenza Dick Band's burden became ever heavier. He worked, ate at odd intervals, slept when he could. Mostly he worked.

The half-formed questions raised by Tom Calindar's death nagged at the back of his mind, though he had little time to consider them. Nor did he find time to ask about the results of any police inquiries into the incident. His formal report had been received without comment, and no questions had followed. His first reaction when he was requested to attend the inquest was one of irritation. Luckily the coroner was to sit in Colombury, in a room in the town hall, which at least saved a journey to Oxford. Band arrived late.

The room which had been allotted for the purpose of the inquest was small, as it had not been anticipated that the inquiry would attract much interest, since the verdict was virtually a foregone conclusion. Dick Band, sidling quietly through the door, was surprised to find so many people and so many heads turned in his direction. He sensed they were awaiting his arrival.

'Ah, Dr Band.' The coroner greeted him at once. 'You have appeared at an appropriate moment. Doubtless you were detained by other pressing business—the demands of your practice, perhaps. We have gone ahead without the advantage of your testimony. Perhaps we may be permitted to hear it now.'

Band, inwardly cursing the pompous man, made his

apologies. He explained succinctly and lucidly how he had been telephoned by Mr Harman and had found Tom Calindar dead on the cellar floor at the manor. He outlined the conclusions he had reached from his preliminary examination, and added that he had made a full written report to the police.

'I have it here, Dr Band,' said the coroner, shuffling his papers. 'You mention that you smelt gin on the body.'

'Yes. That's so.'

'Are you aware that the post mortem examination showed very little alcohol in Mr Calindar's stomach or blood?'

'No, sir. I was unable to attend the post mortem and I haven't seen the report. I can only suggest that in some way Mr Calindar may have spilt gin on himself.'

'Or perhaps you were mistaken, Doctor. The police reports make no mention of a smell of alcohol—other than that which might be expected in a cellar devoted to the storage of liquor. And, as I say, the autopsy proves beyond doubt that Mr Calindar was entirely sober when he met his death.'

There was reproof in the coroner's voice, but Band made no reply.

'Moreover,' the coroner went on, 'Mrs Elizabeth Horton, Mr Calindar's sister, has assured us that her brother never drank gin.'

Again Dr Band made no reply, though he did cast a slightly reproachful glance at Beth Horton. That was not precisely what she had told him, though he had no intention of making a public issue of the point.

'So I'm afraid we shall have to assume that in this instance you *were* mistaken, Dr Band.'

'It's possible, I suppose, though—' Band stopped. The heavy silence in the room had been broken by a loud thud as Diana Poston dropped her handbag. Band watched as she waited for either her husband or her brother, between whom she was sitting, to retrieve it.

Pleased with the doctor's reluctant admission, the coroner allowed him to step down and Band could have left the court then, his duty done, but on impulse he took a vacant seat at the back of the room.

He found himself next to a young woman enveloped in a white fake fur coat that seemed to cover her from throat to slender ankle. Band wondered how she could bear to keep the coat on in this overheated room, but she was clearly very much at ease. As he sat down she turned and gave him a wide, generous smile. A pretty girl, he thought, in spite of somewhat excessive make-up. Expensive too, he added to himself, as her scent wafted over him. He couldn't imagine what she was doing in Colombury in mid-winter, least of all at the inquest of Tom Calindar.

He listened as the coroner summed up the evidence with what seemed to be customary pomposity, brought in a verdict of death by misadventure and expressed his sympathy with the deceased's sister, Mrs Elizabeth Horton. Everyone stood as the coroner departed, and then the audience—if that was the right word—began to file out, some of them seemingly in a hurry to get on with the day's business, others ready to stop for a chat.

Dick Band was anxious to have a word with Beth before he left, so he waited until the group of those around her, offering condolences, had thinned. He noticed that neither of the Postons made any attempt to speak to her. They were moving towards the door now, Diana in the lead, Alan following.

Beside him a husky voice said softly, 'Excuse me, please,' and Band stood back to allow the girl who had been sitting next to him to pass. There wasn't a great deal of room, and she steadied herself by catching his arm as she went by, giving him another wide smile. She was a tall girl, and their faces were almost level. He felt the fur of her collar tickle his skin. Then she was past him and in the aisle.

She reached the door at the same time as Diana Poston

and, watching with amusement, Band saw the two women eye each other appraisingly. But it was only for a moment. Diana—confident in her full-length mink, Band thought—assumed that she had precedence and swept through the doorway, while the girl took a step back.

What happened next seemed to Band somewhat mystifying, if not outright bizarre.

Alan Poston had become separated from his wife during the general movement towards the exit. While the girl waited, the Harmans and another couple followed Diana. Alan came after them, head down, shoulders hunched, his big black coat making him look like some amiable bear.

'Hi, there!'

The girl had moved quickly into the aisle in front of Alan Poston, and was holding her arms wide as if to embrace him. Startled, Alan gave her one wild glance and turned, only to find his way blocked by Guy Frint. Swinging round again, he frowned fiercely at the girl and made to push past her. She was having none of this.

'Surprised to see me?' she asked, standing her ground before him.

'Why—er—yes,' Alan said. 'How are you? Long time no see, what?'

He was still frowning, and Band got the impression he was now trying to convey some message to the girl. It was perhaps unfortunate that Diana had realized that Alan was no longer immediately behind her, and had returned through the now thinning crowd to see what had happened to him. Alan had no alternative; in spite of his obvious reluctance, he was forced to introduce the two women.

'Di, this is Nancy—er—Miss Naury. Old friend—sort of —from London.' He gestured at Diana. 'My wife. Mrs Alan Poston.' He pronounced the last words very clearly.

'Hi!' Miss Naury said, and produced her wide smile again. 'Nice to meet you, Mrs Poston.'

'How do you do,' Diana said coldly. She allowed her hand

to be held for a brief moment. 'Are you staying long in Colombury, Miss Naury?'

'No. I don't suppose so,' the girl said. 'Not more than a couple of days. The Windrush Arms is a quaint old pub, but judging by last night the beds aren't that comfortable.'

Diana nodded. 'Well, we must go. We seem to be obstructing the traffic; Dr Band is trying to get by.' She glanced at Band as if she had just realized he was there. 'Goodbye, Miss Naury.'

''Bye, Mrs Poston.' The girl turned to Alan, looking him full in the face. 'And 'bye—er—Alan. Fancy bumping into you like this. Be seeing you again.'

'Yes, sure,' Alan Poston said weakly.

Mary Band regarded her husband with some exasperation. It was nine o'clock that evening, and he was pushing his food around his plate with a singular lack of interest. She had to admit it didn't look very tempting, but that wasn't her fault. The meat pie had been sitting in the oven for the past two hours, gently drying out while it awaited the doctor's return.

'If you go on like this you'll be ill yourself soon,' she said.

'I'm all right.' Band pushed the plate away from him. 'The pie's fine, Mary, but I'm not hungry.'

'Some cold meat and salad?'

'No. Thanks, darling, but—'

'Then what, Dick? You must have something.'

'I know—cheese. A bit of that Stilton if there's any left, and some coffee.'

'Right.'

Mary busied herself getting his snack. But the Bands had been married for twenty years and by now Mary knew her husband pretty well. She had a good idea what was to happen. Cheese and coffee were not to be recommended for a tired man, unless he wanted to talk. In spite of his seemingly calm exterior she was aware—had been aware for days—that something was worrying him, something was nagging at the back of his mind. And from odd remarks he'd let drop she had a fair idea of what the problem might be. It was that business of Tom Calindar, she thought to herself.

She brought the cheese and made the coffee, and sat at the table with her husband. She listened in silence while he told her of his doubts about Tom Calindar's death.

'But who would want Tom dead?' she asked reasonably when he had finished.

'I know. I know.' Band was irritable. 'Do you think I haven't asked myself that over and over again? When Beth told me, as I understood it, that he got a kick from gin, I was prepared to rationalize the situation, to believe he'd been trying to get tight. Now she says she didn't mean it like that. She meant that gin made him so unwell he hasn't drunk it for years, and wasn't likely to.'

'She might not know,' Mary objected. 'He could have started drinking again.'

'Why, if it upset him? There was plenty of whisky available, I assume.'

Mary Band sighed. 'Still, it's only the gin that makes you—'

'That damned coroner implied I was suggesting that Tom fell down those stairs because he was drunk, and one shouldn't speak ill of the dead, or something,' Band interrupted irritably. 'I thought inquests were meant to search for truth, not just confirm people's preconceived ideas. But the man practically forced me to admit I could have been mistaken—and I suppose I could.'

'But you don't believe you were—are?' Mary gave her husband an affectionate look. 'In which case,' she added when he didn't answer, 'there's only one thing you can do. Take Superintendent Thorne out to lunch and discuss the matter with him.'

Dick Band grinned. 'Excellent advice, as always,' he said.

CHAPTER 12

The headquarters of the Thames Valley Police is located at Kidlington, just outside Oxford, but for reasons of space one of the Force's two Serious Crime Squads is based in Bicester, a town some ten miles north-east of the headquarters. It was here that Dick Band phoned Detective-Superintendent Thorne the next morning, and invited him to lunch at the Windrush Arms in Colombury.

George Thorne knew Band well, and had come to like and respect him as a most efficient police surgeon and a kind and humane man, but his first inclination had to be to refuse with regret, at least for the next few days or weeks. Winter sickness was rife among the police, as well as in Colombury. The Serious Crime Squad was at present under-staffed and overworked. If he took time off for lunch out of town, he would almost certainly have to make it up by staying late at the office to cope with his paperwork, and there had been too many late nights recently; it wasn't fair on Miranda, his wife, he thought.

'I'm terribly sorry,' he began.

'—today, if you possibly could,' said the voice on the phone. 'I should really be extremely grateful.'

Thorne thought for a moment, and changed his mind. This was obviously a good deal more than a simple social invitation. Band wouldn't invite him to lunch in terms like these without a good reason.

'All right then,' he said. 'Twelve-thirty today. The Wind-rush Arms. I'll be there. Thanks.'

He put down the receiver but was still staring at the phone when Detective-Sergeant Abbot came into the room. Abbot had been born and brought up in Colombury, and the Superintendent, himself an import from London, had learnt to appreciate the fact that the Sergeant was a good and reliable source of local rumour and information.

'Bill, tell me,' he said affably as Abbot handed him a couple of files, 'have there been any untoward happenings in your part of the world in the last few weeks?'

'Untoward happenings, sir?' Thorne didn't often call the Sergeant by his first name, and Abbot was immediately a little on the defensive. 'In Colombury, you mean?'

'Or round and about there. Yes.'

For a moment Abbot remained dubious; he was never absolutely sure about his Super's motives. Then his natural cheerfulness asserted itself and he grinned. 'The usual crop of crimes, sir, as far as I know, and doubtless even more unreported sin, but nothing—nothing especially untoward, I'd say. There was Sir Oliver Poston, the elderly financial wizard. He died the other week, but that was obviously natural causes; it had been expected for ages. You must have read about it, sir.'

'Ah yes, I did.' Thorne nodded. 'It was in all the papers. A great deal of money involved, as I recall.' And how often money and crime go together, he reflected unoriginally. 'That's all? You can't think of anything else?'

Abbot hesitated, but then he added, 'Well, it seems that the night of Sir Oliver's funeral, his old servant—a chap called Tom Calindar—who'd looked after the old man for years, managed to fall down some cellar steps in Sir Oliver's house and kill himself. Probably drunk, if you ask me. Dr Band was police surgeon and he as good as hinted at it at the inquest, but the PM findings didn't support him and the coroner wasn't having any. I could easily find the report on the inquest if you're interested, sir.'

'No, no, leave it,' Thorne said, dismissing the subject with a nod and turning his attention to the file on his desk. As Abbot was leaving the office he added, 'Dr Band's invited me to lunch over in Colombury today. I'll probably be a bit late back.'

'Very good, sir,' Abbot said. But he thought: You cunning old devil, so that's why you've been asking all these questions. 'I hope you enjoy yourself, sir,' he said, his face perfectly straight, as he opened the door.

While Superintendent Thorne and Sergeant Abbot were considering lunch, Nancy Naury was just finishing the breakfast that had been sent up to her room at the Windrush Arms. Normally she was a cheerful, carefree girl, but today she was feeling puzzled, and vaguely depressed. There were things she didn't understand.

She had waited up till nearly midnight before retreating alone to her uncomfortable bed. She had been so sure that Alan Poston—her dear 'Hen', as she'd known him in London—would visit her, if only for a short while, but there had been no sign of him. She supposed it was because of Mrs Diana. When she decided to come down to Colombury, she hadn't even known that Henry had a wife. Thinking about it as she ate the last piece of toast, she realized that there was quite a lot she hadn't known about Henry Logan.

Nancy had first met Henry Logan by chance in London the previous spring, and had immediately been attracted to him. A most enjoyable relationship had lasted well into the summer. But it had ended abruptly. Henry had suddenly announced that 'a family matter' had arisen, and he wouldn't be able to see her for some time.

Nancy had had no choice but to accept this brush-off. She'd wept a few tears and resigned herself to the inevitable, though she had a very soft spot for 'Hen'. It was hard to get used to the idea of him as Alan, she thought. Anyway, for a while she had hoped he'd return, but when the months passed and she heard nothing she did her best to forget him.

Then, a few days ago, idly turning the pages of a glossy magazine, she'd come across a photograph of one Alan Poston who, according to the caption, had recently inherited the bulk of the estate of his father, multi-millionaire financier

Sir Oliver Poston. Nancy had stared at the picture in amazement. It was an old one, clearly taken some years ago, and he looked younger than she remembered him, but it was undoubtedly her 'Hen'.

Nancy Naury had never heard of Oliver Poston and she'd had no idea that her old boyfriend was in line to inherit a fortune. Certainly he'd never mentioned it. But now she thought she knew what he'd meant by 'a family matter'.

Curious, Nancy went to the public library and looked up Sir Oliver Poston. She learned two things that interested her. One was that Sir Oliver's second name was Henry, the other his address in the Cotswolds. She looked for a separate entry on Alan Poston, but found none.

Nancy Naury was not an avaricious woman. She liked expensive clothes. She would have loved to have lots of money, to have married a millionaire. But she'd turned down the only one who had ever proposed to her. Alan Poston—her 'Hen'—was a different matter. She'd been really fond of him, and she believed it was mutual. Almost on impulse she decided to visit the Cotswolds, and ask around.

Hence her presence at the inquest on Tom Calindar. But the existence of Diana Poston had been a shock to her—as had Henry's odd behaviour after the inquest, though she thought she understood that: the situation was embarrassing, to say the least. The presence of a wife also explained why he'd felt it necessary to give himself a different name; that hurt a little, for surely he must have known she'd understand. Anyway, she had fully expected him to visit her or contact her at the Windrush Arms.

It was sad but true that he'd done neither, and Nancy knew when to cut her losses. After breakfast, she took a long bath, packed her weekend bag, paid her bill, collected her car and drove back to London. She missed Alan Poston by about forty minutes.

★

Alan arrived at the Windrush Arms shortly before noon. He was not alone; Guy, his brother-in-law, was with him, and it would have been clear to any interested observer that they were both ill-tempered. They went into the bar just off the reception hall, and Alan immediately ordered a double whisky, drank it down and ordered another. Guy was still on his first gin.

'For God's sake, don't get stoked, Alan,' he said angrily.

Alan gave him a mean glance. 'I can't think of any other reason for being in this pub,' he said. 'I've told you. Nancy Naury was just a girl I picked up in London a few weeks ago and slept with a few times. Hell, I can't live like a monk, and Di's no use to me. Tony gives her all she wants.'

'Don't be so damned crude,' Guy said. He sipped his gin reflectively. 'And that's not the point, as you bloody well know. If she was only a pick-up, what the hell's she doing down here?'

'A few days' holiday in the Cotswolds? Why not?'

'In December?' Guy laughed. 'Don't be stupid. From what I saw of her, your ex-girlfriend didn't look like an outdoors type. And that wouldn't account for her being at the inquest.'

Alan Poston stared into his glass. He was worried as hell, but he had no idea what to do about the situation. After the inquest, Diana and Guy and Tony had questioned him about his relationship with Nancy, and he'd lied his head off because there had seemed no option. Now in all likelihood his bluff was going to be called. He looked anxiously towards the reception desk.

'What do we do—stay here all day?' he asked peevishly. 'Nancy could have gone into Oxford—gone anywhere.'

'Perhaps,' Guy said. 'Of course we could ask if she's in the hotel, but we want to try and meet her casually.'

Alan shrugged. 'I don't see the point,' he said.

'Don't you?' Guy smiled enigmatically. 'Then you must be a fool, Alan.'

Alan ignored the remark. 'Why couldn't I have come to see her by myself?'

'Because Di doesn't trust you, not a hundred per cent.' Guy grinned suddenly. 'Can you blame her?'

Alan didn't answer. He finished his drink and signalled to the barman for a refill. He wished now that he'd been frank about Nancy. After all, he thought, if he'd told the truth there was nothing Diana or any of them could have done. As it was— He cursed himself for not having reacted more sensibly.

It was shortly after twelve-thirty when Dick Band looked into the bar, now filling up with lunch-time drinkers. He glanced round, said hello to one or two friends, nodded at Alan Poston and Guy Frint, and went out again. He was late, but he was relieved to see that the Superintendent had not yet arrived. He sat in the hall, where he could keep an eye on the front door of the hotel, and waited, desultorily glancing through the pages of someone's discarded morning paper.

Five minutes later Alan and Guy came out of the bar, Alan slightly unsteady on his feet. He slumped into a chair close to Band, without noticing him. Guy went to the reception desk. Almost at once he returned to Alan, and Band couldn't help but overhear their conversation.

'She's gone,' Guy said. 'Cleared out this morning.'

'She has? Good—oh!' Alan was suddenly cheerful. 'You see, I was right. Coincidence. Bit of a holiday, that's all. Nothing to do with me at all. Just chance she bumped into us.'

'Maybe. Come on. Let's go.'

'What's the hurry? If I'd not insisted on inquiring we'd have been here all day.'

Nevertheless, Alan pushed himself out of his chair, and followed Guy. Band watched them with interest. Though no name had been mentioned, he had no doubt they'd been talking about Miss Nancy Naury of the wide smile. He wondered what they wanted with her. Then he was distracted by the sight of Alan Poston colliding with Superintendent Thorne in the main doorway. He got up to greet his guest.

George Thorne apologized for being late, blaming a conference with his Chief Constable. He at once agreed to go straight into the dining-room, where Band's favourite corner table had been reserved for them. They ordered drinks and then, while they waited for their food to come, talked casually but in patches.

Dick Band was beginning to have doubts. Glancing at the trim figure opposite him the doctor was less than encouraged. Thorne, he thought, looked more like an army major or an old-style district commissioner than a senior police officer. He was unlikely to be thanked for wasting the Superintendent's time.

Then Thorne looked up from his soup, his grey eyes amused. 'Come on,' he said. 'Spill the beans. Tell me what's worrying you. You know you're going to. Maybe I can help and maybe I can't, but it won't do any harm to talk it over.'

Band grinned, his doubts suddenly resolved. 'You've heard of Sir Oliver Poston—' he began, then broke off. 'Incidentally, that was his son and heir, Alan, who nearly knocked you down as you were coming into the pub just now.'

'The chap with the mane of hair and those extraordinary eyebrows?' Thorne asked.

Band nodded, and when the Superintendent acknowledged that he had heard of the Postons, continued, 'Well it's really a man called Tom Calindar I want to talk to you about. For years Calindar was Sir Oliver's personal servant and general factotum—he was originally Sir Oliver's batman in World War Two, I think. Anyway, they'd been together a very long time, and they were more like old friends than master and servant. Tom was a good man, devoted—'

Thorne listened attentively as the doctor proceeded with his tale. When it was finished he asked a few questions, but not many. Band had told the story—almost made a statement—well; he'd done his best to fill in the background completely, and describe the persons involved, as well as explain his misgivings. Indeed, Thorne was surprised at how much seemingly irrelevant material about Sir Oliver Poston and his ménage, and the inhabitants of the lodge and their relationships and their friends and activities the doctor had managed to acquire. It was an impressive performance, but it was useless, at least as the situation stood at present.

Regretfully the Superintendent began to tell Band what he guessed the doctor already knew. Suspicions were not enough. The inquiry, such as it had been, was closed, and new facts were needed if any further investigation was to be commenced—facts, hard evidence, and above all pointers to a motive. Without one or other of these things it was hard to see what official action was possible.

Nevertheless, when Thorne returned to Bicester, he made some very full notes of his lunch-time conversation, and put them in a file in a desk drawer he kept locked.

Part Three

CHAPTER 13

That winter was cold and long in the Cotswolds, and slow
to give way to spring. There were still patches of ice under
the hedgerows as March ended, and the few daffodils that
had been brave enough to flower in St Mary's churchyard
shivered in the chill wind that seemed to blow constantly
from the north.

But eventually, as always, the seasons changed, and April
brought the first real promise of better weather. Now Beth
Horton was able to cycle over from Fairfield to put flowers
on her brother's grave more frequently. Occasionally she
would lay a few blossoms on Sir Oliver's; no one else seemed
to pay it any attention. Though it was always neat and tidy
—James Worth, the chief executor, had made provision for
that—it remained, as the Reverend Simon Kent was wont
to comment, 'unloved'. Alan Poston never came near it.

The passing months were frustrating for the Postons.
Urged on by Diana, Alan expostulated time and time again
over the delay in obtaining probate for Sir Oliver's will,
but his efforts got nowhere. The seemingly endless legal
procedures took their course, and James Worth refused to
nudge at them, steadily maintaining that interference with
the law's delay would be counter-productive. Nor did Worth
go out of his way to be helpful to the Postons by authorizing
advances before probate or assisting them to borrow against
their expectations.

Alan continued to receive his allowance, but the extra
gifts that Sir Oliver had provided at Christmas and birthday

were no longer forthcoming. The London flat and the lodge were available always, but, to Diana's chagrin, James Worth refused to sanction any move to the manor; there the Harmans remained as custodians, the house unused.

With the promise of so much to come, the not inconsiderable sums to which Alan and Diana had access seemed less and less adequate, and they began to quarrel seriously about money. Diana complained about the amounts Alan seemed to fritter away, especially in London. Alan pointed to Guy's gambling and the presents Diana gave to Tony Dinsley.

They quarrelled, too, as was to be expected, about drink and sex. Diana claimed that Alan was becoming an alcoholic and was away on his own too much. Alan pointed to Tony Dinsley. 'I'm a healthy male animal, and I've got needs,' he would say. 'You satisfy Tony, but you do damn-all for me, so someone else has to. If I want a night out by myself, I'm taking it.'

Diana had no choice but to acquiesce. Once probate had been granted and Alan had come into his inheritance things would change, she told herself. With a good slice of old Sir Oliver's fortune she could really go places with Tony, achieve the ambitions that her marriage to Alan had originally promised. But till then—

Meanwhile, there was one fact about Alan of which Diana was unaware—that on their return to London after Tom Calindar's funeral the previous December Alan had seized the first opportunity to get in touch again with Nancy Naury. He told her a mixture of truths, half-truths and out and out lies, most of which she believed because she wanted to. At least she was sure that soon he would be enormously rich, and she could only hope he meant it when he said that he would then divorce his wife and marry her. She didn't really understand why the start of divorce proceedings had to wait until probate was granted, or why his affair with her had to remain a secret till then, but she was prepared to accept his assurance that 'legal reasons' existed. In the meantime, she enjoyed their current relationship.

There were other factors that had their effect on the Postons' group. Tony Dinsley had recently learnt that a certain Member of Parliament was about to retire on grounds of ill-health, and that Central Office would support him if he chose to apply for the prospective parliamentary candidacy. He was unlikely to be elected—the constituency had always been marginal for his party—but Tony knew that if he turned down this unexpected opportunity he would be looked upon less favourably in the future. There was no doubt it was a big chance. Now was the time to wine and dine people of influence, to be seen in the right places, to gain the confidence of the media. Unfortunately such activities needed money, of which he was woefully short. Diana was as generous as she could be, but her contributions were nowhere near what was required.

Guy and Frank Leder also had their problems. Guy had abandoned even a pretence of work in favour of gambling, and clearly this activity wasn't going as well as it might. He had no steady girlfriend, and he now spent his time almost entirely with the Postons and Tony Dinsley. Leder was worried about his business. Expansion was essential if it were to succeed, and now was the crucial moment.

It was a curious situation. Diana, Tony and Guy were a close-knit group—even closer than they had been before Alan's accident. Alan and Frank were, in different ways, on the fringes, but nevertheless dependent on the kernel. But as a group they were much less gregarious than they had been. Now there were no big noisy parties at the Postons' flat or at the lodge; their hospitality was noticeably limited.

And, what was more unusual, they all stayed in England. There was no skiing in Switzerland that January, no visit to the south of France at Easter, no spring cruises. They were waiting—waiting for probate—and they wanted to be right on the spot when it was finally granted.

★

Frank Leder's death was probably inevitable in the long run—the killer was growing more greedy—but to some extent he precipitated it himself.

That year Easter was late—at the end of April. The Postons went down to the lodge for the long weekend. As usual, they were joined by Guy and Tony; Celia remained in France. On the Saturday Frank drove over with Kathleen, who had been persuaded somewhat against her will to accompany him for once.

It was a day of sullen grey skies and steady drizzle, interspersed with heavier showers. For some reason—probably the continuing damp weather—the sitting-room chimney at the lodge had started to smoke, which made a fire almost impossible. The central heating kept the house warm enough, but the atmosphere was cheerless, to say the least.

The obvious result was that they drank even more than usual before and during lunch and then found themselves at the loosest of loose ends. Television, a video movie, bridge, strip poker—Alan's suggestion, instantly vetoed by Kathleen—nothing seemed worth the effort. The afternoon stretched ahead like a bog of boredom, until it would be time to start drinking again.

'What we need,' said Guy finally, 'is a good country walk. Air and exercise, that's the thing. Give us an appetite for dinner.'

'In this weather?' Tony was disgusted.

'If only the blasted fire would burn properly,' Diana said, poking at a log and producing a cloud of smoke that made her cough. 'You'd think the Harmans would manage to see to it that our fire works. Instead, they sit up there at the manor doing damn-all.' She added irritably, 'They're paid enough.'

It was the mention of the manor that gave Kathleen Leder the idea. 'I suppose—' she began tentatively, and when everyone looked at her continued more eagerly, 'I suppose we couldn't go up there—to the manor, I mean. I've never seen over the whole place and it's something I've always wanted to do. There are some fine things to see, aren't there? Paintings and—'

'The best of the paintings have gone,' Diana interrupted, 'and so's anything else of any value. Put in a bank vault for safe-keeping by our dear James Worth—'

'But that's a splendid suggestion.' The words were slurred.

Diana glanced up quickly. In her turn she had been interrupted by Frank Leder. She regarded him with some disgust. Though she drank plenty herself, she had a rooted dislike for men who couldn't hold their liquor, and Leder had never been one of her favourite people on those grounds alone. She wondered if he—and Kathleen?—had some special reason for wanting to visit the manor, and decided that Frank was probably merely trying to placate his wife.

'Why not?' Guy was saying.

Diana shrugged. 'Why not?' she repeated. 'Anything's better than sitting here glooming. Okay. Let's go.' For a moment she considered phoning to warn the Harmans, but she decided against it. If the bloody Harmans were annoyed, so much the better, she thought.

Some twenty minutes later they arrived at the manor, a rather bedraggled crew. Raincoated and booted, sheltering under umbrellas, they had walked up from the lodge in a steady downpour. Mrs Harman opened the door to them, and clearly showed her surprise.

'We've come to show some friends over the house,' Diana said firmly.

Mrs Harman hesitated, then decided she had no option but to acquiesce. 'Very good, madam,' she said.

She watched, apparently impassive, as they trudged in, ignoring the pools of water and the dirty footmarks they were making on the highly-polished parquet flooring in the hall. They put down their umbrellas and stripped off their raincoats. Harman, who had appeared from the servants' quarters, allowed himself to be laden with the sodden objects, his face as stony as his wife's.

Mr Worth had said that, if they encountered trouble of any kind, they were to report to him, but so far, apart from an occasional tour of inspection by Diana alone, the Postons hadn't come near the manor. Now, suddenly presented with a somewhat drunken, obviously careless collection of visitors, the Harmans were unsure what action to take. They muttered together for a few moments, then Harman retreated to the rear premises with the dripping garments and Mrs Harman followed the Postons and their friends at a respectful distance.

The party made a thorough inspection of the place, stripping dust-covers from the furniture and passing small pieces from one to another. Kathleen Leder was particularly enthusiastic, ready to admire everything and laughing away the marks on the walls where pictures had formerly hung and the obvious absence of many *objets d'art* from the bare shelves and display cabinets. 'You're a lucky woman, Di,' she said. 'You really are.'

Diana smiled, taking the remark as a compliment. 'I'll feel even luckier when that man Worth gets off the pot and does his job, and I know it really is all mine.'

'Don't you mean mine, Di, love?' Alan demanded, emphasizing the term of affection. 'Your dear husband's. That's whose it really is—or will be soon. Aren't you forgetting? Dad didn't leave you a brass farthing. It was me he left it all to, remember?'

Diana's sharp breath hissed between her teeth as Alan gave a great guffaw of laughter. The laughter ended abruptly as she turned and smacked him sharply across the face. She was shaking with anger.

'You bloody fool!' she said. 'If it wasn't for me you wouldn't be—'

'Di!'

It was Guy who uttered the exclamation, but it was Tony who went to Diana. He gathered her into his arms for a brief moment, then shook her lightly. Diana responded, gaining control of her temper almost at once.

'Sorry,' she said. 'Sorry, Alan.' She looked behind her to where Mrs Harman hovered in the doorway; later, Mrs Harman was to describe to her husband the look on Diana's face as one of pure venom. Diana turned back to Alan. 'Forgive?' she said, with a forced smile.

'But of course, Di.' Alan replied at once, though there was still an edge in his voice. 'All is forgiven, sweetie. We know the form.'

It was then that Frank Leder made his fatal intervention.

In fact, given the circumstances, it was not unreasonable: he was desperately worried about his company's need to expand and the sources of finance for such an operation and, what was more, he'd had far too much to drink in the course of the day. Though like the others he'd been inside the manor before, this was the first opportunity he'd had to inspect the place thoroughly. He had been following the tour with a knowledgeable and appraising eye. Even with the major valuables removed, the house and its remaining contents were enough to whet his envy.

'I should damn well think so,' he said loudly, 'and the sooner I get my share the better.'

'Your share?' Alan laughed.

'Yes, Alan. My share. What you promised me. What you agreed. And considering how much you're going to get, I think you could easily up it a bit.'

'Me? *I* promised you nothing, Frank.' Alan was no longer laughing.

'Well, Di, then. What we agreed.'

'For heaven's sake, Frank!' Kathleen protested. 'What are you talking about? We're no relation to Alan and Di, worse luck. Why on earth should you expect to share their good—'

Leder shrugged off the restraining hand that his wife had put on his arm. 'Why? Because it was agreed, that's why. Otherwise I'd never—never have—' His voice trailed away into nothingness.

'Never what?' Kathleen said quietly.

'He's tight, Kath,' Guy said. 'Pay him no attention.'

'Tight as a coot,' Tony joined in.

'But it's true we did promise,' Diana said. By now she had quite recovered her composure and was fully conscious of Mrs Harman within earshot. 'It was perfectly reasonable. After all, even if Frank isn't a relation, he's a very old school chum of Alan's. As soon as it's possible we'll put the money we agreed upon into his firm.'

'Lots of it,' Frank said. 'Lots of it. The bloody firm needs it. You'll put in what I need—and that's a hell of a lot of money. Otherwise—'

'Otherwise, what?' Alan asked.

'Otherwise—' Frank Leder, perhaps feeling himself threatened by Alan, took a step backwards and collided with a small pedestal table. Caught off balance he involuntarily sat heavily upon it. The table collapsed beneath his weight. Everyone laughed. And Frank, by the time he was on his feet again, had forgotten what he'd been talking about.

CHAPTER 14

Although the decision that Frank Leder must die was taken that rainy day in April, he had some weeks' respite. His death did not in fact take place until mid-June. The delay was because the arrangements needed careful thought and planning. Unlike Sir Oliver Poston, Frank Leder was a strong, healthy man, who wouldn't easily succumb to a sudden attack of any kind that could reasonably be made to appear natural. Some sort of accident was considered and discarded. Tom Calindar's death couldn't be copied; that had been an improvisation, necessarily hurried once it seemed that he was becoming suspicious, and it had not been without potentially dangerous consequences.

The murderer's options were thus limited, and the idea of suicide had the greatest appeal in the circumstances. Leder's business was in difficulty; his shortage of money was well-known; he drank too much and appeared to lead a frantic, unsatisfactory life. He was clearly an ideal candidate for a suicide attempt, but a convincing scenario wasn't the simplest thing in the world to organize. There was no alternative to careful investigation and planning.

By the second week of June, however, the killer was satisfied that all foreseeable eventualities had been considered, and all possible precautions taken. It was perhaps ironic that the day chosen for the execution of the plan was the Thursday on which Sir Oliver Poston's executors were finally granted probate of the old man's will. Leder wasn't given to keeping to a regular schedule, but he was known to try to tidy up his firm's paper work at least once a week, usually on a Thursday; on such a day he was quite likely to be found in his office later than usual.

The killer was lucky. On this particular Thursday Frank Leder's employees, mostly women who spent their time manufacturing beautifully designed, very large and exceedingly expensive stuffed animals, streamed out of the factory at five-thirty in the evening. Leder's secretary was the last to depart, leaving her boss still busy in his office. The killer knew that the night watchman wouldn't come on duty till nine, and that the factory and its offices were cleaned in the early morning rather than at night.

The killer was watching from a car, parked unobtrusively some way along the road. When it was certain that the factory parking lot was empty except for Leder's Jaguar, speed was essential to make sure of forestalling—and then facilitating—Leder's own departure.

The firm's offices were in a wing at one end of the single-storey factory building, and it was possible to see straight through the window into Leder's sanctum, where he sat at his desk. The killer tapped on the glass.

Frank Leder looked up, startled until he saw who it was. Then a series of expressions chased themselves across his face—surprise, pleasure, hope. Grinning, he got to his feet and hurried through his secretary's office and along the corridor to open the outer door to his unexpected guest.

'Hi! This is a nice surprise.'

'Not too unwelcome? Am I disturbing you?'

'Of course not. Come along in. I've about finished as much as I can do. I was just thinking of having a drink before setting off for home.'

'That sounds a splendid idea.'

Leder ushered his visitor into his office. It was a fair-sized room, functionally but pleasantly furnished—desk, large executive chair, side table with a small typewriter, two comfortable armchairs with a coffee table between them in one corner. The walls were painted a buttercup yellow and the curtains, appropriately enough, were a repetitive print of Noah's Ark and its animals. Some of the animals were in the room itself. A full-sized lion lay in front of one of the windows, and in another corner a giraffe's head was touching the ceiling.

'It's ages since you were here, isn't it?' Leder said. 'I've had the office redecorated. Can't really afford it, but one's got to create a good impression on foreign buyers, you know.'

'Yes.'

The single monosyllable seemed to disconcert Frank Leder. 'I got a good order today from a German chap,' he

said a little defensively, 'and he's interested in this—I hope
it's going to be a good new line.' He picked up a smaller
stuffed animal from his desk and held it out. 'What do you
think of him? He'll be at least four times this size when he's
made up properly, of course.' Leder spoke with a curious
affection which surprised his visitor.

'A unicorn!' There was amusement in the visitor's voice.
'I like it. Maybe you've got a best-seller there.'

'And just at the right time,' Leder said. 'If only I could
get my hands on some of Sir Oliver's money and expand
immediately.' For a moment he looked doubtful. Then he
grinned. 'Or is that why you're here? About the money?'

'You could say so, yes.'

'Great!' Leder waved towards the armchairs by the coffee
table. 'Sit down and tell me. But first I'll get us a drink.
What'll it be? Whisky? Gin? I've most things.'

'Whisky and water, please. No ice.'

'Right.' Leder went to a door which opened to reveal a
small bar with a sink and a refrigerator built into a cupboard.
He poured the drinks; the murderer was glad to see he made
them strong, but not too long. He set the glasses on the table
between the two chairs. 'Now,' he said expectantly, making
to sit down.

A gesture stopped him. 'Frank, do you have your trading
figures for the first quarter of the year?'

'What? My accounts, you mean?' Leder was obviously
surprised, but he replied, 'Sure. They'll be on file, in my
secretary's room.'

'Could I see them?'

'You? Why on earth should you want—'

'Frank, please. I've come to discuss money, remember.
Worth got probate today, and maybe if you could explain
what you really need and why, we—'

'He did? Probate—at last?' The news inspired Leder, and
his face broke into a huge smile. 'I see what you mean.
Okay, why not? There's no reason why you shouldn't see

the figures. You're hardly likely to become a competitor.' He laughed. 'Hang on a minute.'

Leder went through to his secretary's office. He left the door between the rooms ajar, and the sounds of him opening and shutting the drawers of a filing cabinet were loud. The killer had enough time. It took only a moment to pour the contents of a small bottle into Frank Leder's whisky. It made no difference to its appearance, and he wouldn't be given the time to notice any odour.

As Frank Leder returned and put down a bulky file on the coffee table, the murderer was already proposing a toast. 'To you, Frank, and to all our futures! And to the new product!'

'To all our futures! Cheers!'

Frank Leder took the unicorn in one hand, seized his glass in the other and drank the whisky at a gulp. The poison diffused rapidly through his system, and in but a few seconds he had dropped his glass and fallen to his knees, his hands clutching at his throat. As his breathing slowed, his face contorted with the effort of struggling to stay alive and he uttered inarticulate sounds. A blue tinge appeared on his lips and spread across his face. Suddenly his body convulsed twice in rapid succession, and then lay still. The dose had been strong, and its effect was complete in three or four minutes.

The murderer, restraining an instinct to panic and flee, knelt beside Leder, to examine the body, placing fingers over the carotid arteries and listening with ear to chest for any sign of a heartbeat. Finally satisfied, the killer slipped on a pair of gloves and went to the small typewriter by Leder's desk, inserted a sheet of paper and typed:

Dear Kathleen.
I can't go on any longer. Everything's become too much for me. I'm sorry, love.

Frank.

Leaving the paper in the machine and Leder's glass on the carpet beside his outflung arm, the murderer picked up the second glass, rinsed it at the bar sink, dried it and replaced it on the shelf above. Then there was nothing more to do. With a careful glance around the scene to check that all was in order, Frank Leder's killer slipped unseen out of the building.

As usual the night watchman appeared at nine o'clock. He was a conscientious man and invariably his first action was to make a thorough inspection of the premises. He usually left the office wing till last but tonight, seeing that the boss's car was still in its parking place and a light still on in his office, he did what Leder's murderer had done and peered through the window on his way into the building. Mr Leder was presumably working late, and if so he would take care not to disturb him.

His immediate impression was that the office was empty, but at a second glance he saw his employer on the carpet, over by the coffee table in the corner. He raced for the door, assuming that Leder had been taken ill—a heart attack, maybe. It wasn't until he was in the room and had inspected the contorted face and the twisted body that he knew Leder was dead. As he made for the phone he saw the letter in the typewriter.

He dialled '999' and spoke to the police.

Detective-Superintendent Thorne stood in a corner of Frank Leder's office, keeping out of the way of the half-dozen experts who were measuring, photographing, dusting for fingerprints. It was a rule that all but the most obvious cases of apparent suicide should be investigated thoroughly, and the Superintendent had been at Bicester when the call had come through from Colombury. The name of Leder had struck a chord from the notes he had made after his lunch with Dick Band weeks ago, and Thorne had decided to come and have a look at the situation for himself.

On his arrival he had found Band with the body, in his capacity as police surgeon. The doctor had wasted no time, and had made no reference to their earlier conversation. 'We'll know for sure after the PM, but I don't think there's any doubt. Poison—and some form of cyanide, for a cert. The face is cyanosed, and there's still a bit of an almond smell around and in that glass. It looks as if he took it in whisky. No signs of struggle, as far as I can see.'

'A painful way to do away with yourself, I should have thought.'

'Very. But quick and certain. Guns are hard to get hold of and messy; a mistake can have ghastly consequences. The good old overdose is all very well, but interfering types have a habit of finding you too soon and pumping out your stomach. Which just about leaves cutting your throat or your wrists, or jumping off something. Both take more guts than a simple drink.'

Thorne's expression was sombre as he recalled Band's words. Cynical they might have sounded, but there was an element of truth in them. There was no doubt that cyanide was an effective method of suicide. And Leder had left the obligatory note of explanation. Nevertheless—

Absent-mindedly Thorne stroked the giraffe's neck. He was trying to put himself in Frank Leder's place and visualize what might have happened.

First, the decision to kill himself. Why? The note was totally uninformative, but doubtless it would be amplified and supported in due course and reasons would emerge. The file of accounts on the coffee table suggested that money might have been involved. Then he had obtained the poison. Where? Cyanide wasn't all that easy to come by, though it was used in many industrial and manufacturing processes. But stuffed animals? It was a point that must be looked into. Anyway, Leder had got hold of some, which presumably indicated a modicum of advance planning.

Leder had obviously chosen his time carefully, after his work force had gone home and before the night watchman came on duty. He had typed a note to his wife—Band had confirmed that her name was Kathleen—and had left it in the typewriter. Why hadn't he ripped it out and signed it properly. There was something cold and unloving about the typed name at the end of such a letter. But then, Thorne told himself, maybe Leder hadn't loved his wife. Their relationship must also be examined.

Then, note typed, he had gone to the bar in the cupboard, poured himself a whisky, added the poison and—No! He hadn't downed it there and then. The position of the body showed that he had walked over to the set-piece of coffee table and armchairs before he drank. Why? So that he could sit down and die in relative comfort? But he hadn't. There was no doubt he'd taken his medicine standing up, and apparently holding a small stuffed unicorn. Surely there was something wrong or odd here.

Thorne shook himself. These were mere fancies. He was letting his imagination run riot. It was all right for Dick Band to have a funny internal feeling about the death of Tom Calindar, but not appropriate for detective-superintendents to harbour unwarranted suspicions over clear cases of suicide. There were apparently no signs of struggle on the body, and certainly the room wasn't disordered. How could anyone have persuaded Leder to drink a whisky and cyanide cocktail without using force? It wasn't really within the bounds of possi-bility. And yet the very certainty of cyanide made it a useful choice for a murderer who had decided upon poison, but was known to his victim and thus couldn't risk a mistake or—

Thorne shook himself again as Sergeant Abbot appeared from the outer office, looking pleased with himself. 'Sir,' he said, 'I think you should see this.'

'Right.'

Thorne gave the giraffe a final pat and followed Abbot into the adjoining room. Without speaking, the sergeant pointed to a diary lying open on Leder's secretary's desk. It was the kind of office diary that allowed a large space for memoranda against each day, and by the present Thursday had been written, 'Send cheque for two tickets—Grosvenor House ball on 21st. Verify price.' There was a neat tick beside the entry, implying that the task had been completed, and the pencilled notation, '£50'.

Abbot said, 'Who'd spend fifty pounds on tickets for some dance if he knew they'd never be used?'

'I take your point, Abbot.' Thorne nodded. 'He might have told his secretary ages ago, and forgotten. But it's something else to look into.' He pulled at his neat moustache thoughtfully.

CHAPTER 15

Frank Leder's secretary was weeping. She was a matronly woman in the mid-forties, and her tears didn't improve her appearance. Blowing her nose and dabbing at reddening eyes with an inadequate handkerchief, she kept repeating monotonously, 'I can't believe it. I can't believe it.'

'I'm afraid you must, Miss Wilson,' Superintendent Thorne said again gently but firmly. 'Mr Leder is dead and I'm sorry to say there seems every likelihood that he took his own life.'

'No! No!' Miss Wilson said. 'I don't believe it.'

At least this was a slight variation on her theme, Thorne thought. He waited patiently. He realized that she had suffered a severe shock when she arrived at work that morning to find her employer dead, police all over the place and a detective-superintendent installed with his sergeant in her own office. But he wished she would get a grip on her emotions so that he could see if she had anything useful to contribute.

'Why should he have killed himself?' she demanded suddenly, as if the suggestion of suicide was an insult to be resented. 'I don't believe it. I just don't believe it. Mr Leder was a good man. There's no way he'd have done anything like that.'

Thorne suppressed a sigh. It wasn't by any means the first time he had met this obstinate rejection of the idea of suicide, and he could only hope the secretary would eventually produce some sensible reason for her conviction. He decided to change the subject.

'Miss Wilson, I gather you've been Mr Leder's secretary for many years. You probably know the business as well as he did. How's it doing? Well? Or suffering from the recession? Was the firm in financial difficulties? Or Mr Leder himself? We shall find out for ourselves when we go through the books and his papers, but it would save a lot of time and trouble if you'd tell us what the situation is—as you see it, of course.'

Thorne's appeal for her professional advice seemed to restore Miss Wilson's confidence. She blew her nose, dried her eyes, straightened her shoulders and became more like her normal self—the efficient personal secretary. She spoke with an authority and an understanding of the firm's affairs that surprised Thorne, whose suggestion that she was especially well-informed had been merely flattering encouragement.

'—so that's the problem, Superintendent,' she concluded. 'Capital. Sufficient capital. We should have started expanding months ago. It's not too late yet, but it's got to be done soon, or we could go under. But we need more capital. Mr Leder's borrowed all he can, but we're a relatively small supplier to the luxury market, and I'm afraid the banks and the institutions haven't been as helpful as they might.' She shook her head.

'Mr Leder did have money worries, then,' Thorne said, thinking of the file of accounts on the coffee table near the body.

'Yes, but that was nothing new. In fact, I'm sure that recently he was less worried than usual. He told me—in strict confidence—that an old schoolfriend of his was about to come into a great deal of money, and had promised to back him.' Remembering, her face lit up with a smile. 'And he was so pleased about our new prototype—there's a small sample here on my desk—the unicorn; the finished product'll be much larger. Mr Leder hoped it would be a great success. We all did.'

Thorne picked up the unicorn and stroked it ruminatively. He was finding toy animals very pleasant, he thought. He wondered if Miranda would like—Then he brought himself back to the present. 'Did he say who this friend was?' he asked.

Miss Wilson's smile faded and she shook her head. 'Perhaps he let Mr Leder down,' she said sadly, 'and that's why—'

Thorne agreed, glad that Miss Wilson now seemed to accept the situation. 'Perhaps. But Mr Leder was seemingly quite happy when you left him last night? No hint that he might be feeling at the end of his tether?'

'None. On the contrary. Practically the last thing he did was to ask me if I'd remembered to send off the cheque for a charity ball he and his wife—' She broke off as her mood changed again, fresh tears choking her voice. 'I suppose Mr Leder wasn't the world's greatest business man. A small speciality firm like ours needs a lot of time and attention if it's to flourish, and Mr Leder was out of the office too much. It wouldn't be fair to say he neglected it. He didn't. He had lots of bright ideas, and he *wanted* to expand, but there was always something—'

'Other interests got in the way,' Thorne prompted.

Miss Wilson ignored the suggestion. She reverted to her

original theme. 'But I still can't believe he killed himself,' she said. 'I can't believe it. He wasn't that kind of man.' She looked at the closed door that separated her office from Frank Leder's and wept again.

Kathleen Leder was at first similarly positive. 'Frank would never have killed himself,' she said. Then she added, a little illogically, 'What's more, even if he had, it wouldn't have been like that. Frank was a coward—terrified of pain. The only way he could have done it was to get drunk and take an overdose—and he'd probably have had to get so drunk he'd have taken the wrong pills.'

Like Miss Wilson, Mrs Leder had wept—her eyes were red—but the police had of course informed her of her husband's death hours ago, soon after he was found the previous evening. She had had time to get over the first shock, and by now she was feeling angry. She was a conventional woman, and she resented the fact that her husband had apparently died an unconventional death. She resented Superintendent George Thorne. She resented his questions, and the speculative way in which he regarded her. She resented his very presence in her drawing-room, and that of his subordinate—some sergeant taking down every word she uttered.

'Besides,' she said curtly, 'I can't imagine any reason why my husband should have wanted to kill himself. You imply his business isn't doing well, Superintendent. Whose is, at this time? Anyway, I believe he had the situation in hand. I know he had plans to improve matters.'

'With an injection of fresh money from an old school-friend?' Thorne asked blandly.

For a moment Kathleen Leder stared at him, her prominent blue eyes fixed. Then she said acidly, 'You *have* been doing your homework, Superintendent. I suppose you're talking about Alan Poston.'

Thorne nodded, but made no reply and merely waited.

At least he'd learnt something, he thought. So Poston and Leder had been at school together—

'I believe there was some mention of that idea,' Kathleen Leder said. 'But as far as I know nothing definite had been arranged. Now that his father's dead, Alan Poston is a very rich man.'

But would he have been prepared to invest in a firm that was obviously not prospering at present, and not very likely to prosper in the future, at least under Frank Leder's direction, Thorne wondered. Reading between the lines of her comments, Miss Wilson hadn't seemed to think highly of her boss's managerial capabilities, or his capacity for hard work.

Thorne worded his next question carefully. 'I take it that you and your late husband were close friends of the Postons then, Mrs Leder?'

Kathleen Leder hesitated, and her eyes turned from Thorne towards the drawing-room windows and her garden. 'No, Superintendent, I wouldn't say that. Of course Frank had known Alan for a long time, and Frank saw a lot of the Postons—but personally I didn't visit them very often.'

'Why not, Mrs Leder?'

'I think that's my business, Superintendent. What conceivable connection can there be between my social life and my husband's death?'

'I don't know, Mrs Leder,' Thorne replied with complete honesty. 'But if Mr Leder was frequently in the company of people who weren't particular friends of yours, perhaps he had problems of which you knew nothing.'

Kathleen Leder's immediate reaction to this mild comment was anger. 'That seems to me an outrageous suggestion, Superintendent.' Then she paused and stared out of the window again, controlling her temper, and obviously reaching a decision. 'But if you must know, Superintendent,' she said firmly, 'it's true that I'm not especially fond of Alan Poston or his wife. I did try to persuade Frank not to see so

much of them, but he wouldn't listen. He said their way of
life was their own affair, that I was too—too conservative,
too prudish, perhaps—and anyway Alan had always been
a good friend of his.' She turned back to Thorne, clearly
glad to have got that statement off her mind.

But the Superintendent didn't pursue the point. He said,
'You last saw your husband yesterday morning, Mrs Leder?
Or did he come home to lunch?'

'Not yesterday. He was lunching with a prospective client
—from Germany, I think.'

'Did he seem normal—much as usual—when he left
home?'

'Yes. He was perfectly cheerful, talking about a charity
ball we were hoping to attend in London soon.' Kathleen
Leder's face changed expression. 'In a party with the Postons, needless to say.'

'That was one of the slight inconsistencies, Mrs Leder,'
Thorne admitted. 'He did get his secretary to send off a
cheque for the tickets.'

'Yes, I know.'

'You know?' The Superintendent was surprised.

'Why not? He phoned me at six yesterday evening. I'm
sure it was six because the regional news had just started
on television. He told me Miss Wilson had ordered the
tickets.'

'He phoned at six, did he?' Thorne said slowly. 'Did he
tell you anything else—about his day or his plans for the
evening, say?'

'Only that he was doing his usual Thursday paper round,
as he called it—Thursday was the day he usually tried to
catch up with the office paper work—and he'd be late
home.' Kathleen Leder took a deep breath and braced
herself. 'A few hours later there was a ring at the door; at
first I thought Frank had forgotten his keys or something.
But there were two police officers—a man and a girl. I
couldn't believe it. Frank had his faults, God knows, but

he'd never have been so—so brutally unkind to me as to—'

The Superintendent gave his sergeant a quick nod, and Abbot made for the door. Kathleen Leder had buried her face in her hands. Thorne sat and watched her impassively, knowing there was nothing he could do to help. And moments later Abbot returned with Kathleen's sister. Fetched the previous night from Oxford, she had been giving the new widow what support she could.

Thankfully the two police officers departed.

'Abbot,' said Superintendent Thorne a trifle peevishly. 'Can you tell me why any case connected with Colombury and its environs—your part of the country—is invariably complex?'

'I didn't know it was, sir,' Abbot said stolidly as he got into the car beside his superior and fastened his seat-belt. 'You mean, you don't think this chap committed suicide?'

'I'd like to be certain.' Thorne sighed. 'It's all right on the surface—a sudden impulse, maybe. But who keeps cyanide to hand just in case he feels like ending it all? And those dance tickets, the phone call to his wife? Why? It was so unnecessary. I know suicides are supposed to be unpredictable in their behaviour, but still—'

Brow furrowed, pulling at his moustache, Thorne sat in the car wrapped in thought. Abbot turned on the ignition in silence. Better, he knew, to leave the Super to himself when he was in one of his brown studies.

Suddenly Thorne straightened himself. 'Well, what are we waiting for?' he demanded.

'Your seat-belt, sir,' Abbot said, without expression. Thorne grunted, but complied. 'And where, sir?' Abbot asked.

George Thorne looked at his watch. 'Time for lunch,' he said. 'Find me one of those pubs you always know about and I'll stand you a pint. Then we'll go and pay a call on these Postons.'

CHAPTER 16

The sound of splashing and laughter from the pool as the police car drew up beside the lodge assured Superintendent Thorne that someone was at home; it also suggested that the inhabitants of the place were not yet aware of their friend Leder's death. Good, thought Thorne. He had seen no easy way of asking Kathleen Leder not to phone the Postons, but had decided to trust to his intuition that she would make a point of avoiding such a call. As for rumours around the area—well, it would be just too bad if they had spread so far so quickly.

The front door was opened to the two police officers by a dark-haired girl in a blue bikini that matched her eyes and revealed a neat figure. Bill Abbot eyed her appreciatively.

Surely too young to be Diana Poston, Thorne thought, but he said enquiringly, 'Mrs Poston?'

'Me? Heavens, no! I'm Celia Frint, Diana's half-sister. Who are you?' She looked them up and down, not bothering to hide her curiosity.

'Detective-Superintendent Thorne and Detective-Sergeant Abbot, Thames Valley Police,' Thorne said formally, producing his warrant card.

'Police?' Celia's first reaction was amusement. 'And you want Di? What's she been doing? Speeding again?'

'Actually we'd like to talk to Mr Alan Poston first, if he's available.'

'Alan?' Her eyes widened, but she showed no concern. 'Okay. Follow me. It's such a wonderful day we've been having lunch in the garden.'

Celia led them through the house and, by way of french windows, outside again and along a short path to the swimming pool. They had a good thirty seconds to appreciate the scene before any attention was being paid to them. Oddly enough it was young Bill Abbot who regarded it with some distaste; almost again his will he found himself thinking it slightly orgiastic. Thorne seemed to take it in his stride.

Giving a fleeting glance at the remains of the lunch laid out on a long wrought-iron table—avocados, fresh salmon, salad, cheeses, fruit and several empty champagne bottles —Thorne concentrated on the people. There were four of them, apart from Celia Frint.

The only one the Superintendent recognized was Alan Poston. He lay on his back on a floating air cushion, which he was gently propelling around the pool with one hand while he balanced a glass of champagne on his hairy chest with the other. The operation seemed to require a great deal of effort and concentration, and to occupy him fully.

Another man, reclining in a canvas chair, was reading a book, apparently completely absorbed. And a third, lying half asleep on a rug spread on the lawn at the pool's edge was having suntan oil slowly and sensuously spread over his back by an older, more voluptuous version of Celia. Indeed, Thorne was startled by the beauty of the woman's face and figure as she got to her feet and, without haste, reached for a robe to cover her naked breasts. So this, he thought, was Diana Poston.

'Who the hell are you?' she said.

Thorne had no chance to reply. Before he could open his mouth Celia announced loudly, 'Police! For Alan.'

The result of her intervention was dramatic. The scene froze in a moment of complete silence. Then Alan Poston, forgetful of the vulnerability of his position on the air cushion, sat up, sending his champagne glass flying. In spite of violent efforts to save himself, he promptly fell into the water.

Meanwhile the man who had been lying on the rug hurriedly rose to his feet. In his haste he knocked over the bottle of oil that Diana had put down on the ground, drenching his swimming trunks with the stuff. He swore loudly. Of the three men, only the one in the chair remained seemingly unperturbed. He shut his book, marking his place carefully, took off the dark glasses he had been wearing and regarded Thorne with raised eyebrows.

'That's Mr Poston—there in the pool.' He indicated Alan, who had come up spluttering and was paddling to the side. 'Mrs Poston. Mr Dinsley beside her. I'm Guy Frint, Mr Poston's brother-in-law. Now perhaps you'll tell us exactly who you are and what you want.'

For the second time Thorne introduced himself and his sergeant, and produced his credentials. With a deceptive mildness that made Abbot suppress a grin he then apologized profusely for disturbing them on such a lovely afternoon.

'But I should be very grateful if you wouldn't mind answering one or two questions,' he continued, looking hopefully at each of them in turn. 'I believe you're all acquainted with a Mr Francis Leder?'

'Frank? Yes of course,' Diana said, and the others, except for Tony Dinsley who was busy mopping the oil from his trunks, nodded.

'What's old Frank been up to?' Alan heaved himself on to the side of the pool. 'He's not robbed a bank, has he?'

'No, sir.' Thorne didn't smile. 'Though you might say we're here in connection with money.'

'Whose money?' Diana asked quickly.

It was an odd question, Thorne thought. The interview —if it could be described as such—was not being simple. He was glad to have an opportunity to meet Frint and Dinsley, but he could have wished the Postons had been alone, or at least that the whole household had been indoors, in a smaller area where it would be less difficult to watch individual reactions. Besides, it was hot standing in the sun.

Thorne was conscious of the thickness of his suit and the restriction of collar and tie.

He said, 'Perhaps we might sit down together.'

'Sit down together?' Diana made it sound like an indecent suggestion. 'You said you just wanted to ask one or two questions.'

'Oh, come on, Di,' Guy said. 'Okay, Superintendent. If you can bear the remains of our lunch we'll pull up some chairs and sit around the table.'

'I'm not sitting anywhere in these filthy trunks.' Tony Dinsley was firm. Without hesitation he stripped them off and held out a hand. 'Towel,' he said. Alan tossed him one. 'Thanks!' he added as he wrapped it round his waist.

Meanwhile Guy and Celia with the help of Sergeant Abbot had moved chairs and done a little to clear some of the debris from the table. Everyone found somewhere to sit. Thorne didn't miss the small, commanding nod that Diana Poston gave her husband.

Alan said, 'Well, Superintendent, here we are. What's all this about old Frank and money? What kind of financial trouble's he got himself into now?'

Thorne judged it best to be abrupt. 'Mr Leder is dead,' he said.

Every face showed shocked surprise. Guy was the first to recover.

'When?' he said. 'How? An accident?'

'Some time yesterday evening,' Thorne began, when Diana interrupted him.

'Yesterday evening!' she said. 'But why didn't we know before? Why didn't Kathleen phone? I must go over there at once.'

'It's all right,' said Thorne. 'Bear with me for a few minutes. Her sister's with her. And as to why she didn't phone here, I've no idea. But I must tell you that it was unlikely to have been an accident. Mr Leder appears to have killed himself. Apparently he took poison.' The Superintendent explained the circumstances briefly.

This time their expressions registered horror and pity. They murmured a chorus of platitudes. It was Celia who commented on Thorne's choice of words.

'You said "appears" and "apparently",' she said with unexpected astuteness. 'Does that mean there's some doubt? Surely a detective-superintendent wouldn't be involved otherwise?'

The others stared at her as Thorne avoided a direct answer. 'No, there's not really any doubt, but these things have to be investigated,' he said. 'Reports, you know, for the inquest,' he added vaguely. 'And his wife says she's certain he'd never have done such a thing, especially in such a way—' He shrugged as if the matter was of slight importance. 'What do you think? You were all friends of his, Mrs Leder said. Do you think he's been depressed recently?'

Celia said she wouldn't know as she'd been in France and had only returned a couple of days ago, but the rest were unanimous: Frank had been much as usual. Diana remarked that she'd felt for a long time he wasn't getting on too well with his wife. Tony volunteered that Frank drank too much. Guy said he was always short of money. But they all agreed that these were perennial problems. They could suggest no special motive for his killing himself at this particular time, and they echoed his wife's opinion that if he were to contemplate suicide a bottle of gin and a bottle of pills were very much his most likely accompaniments.

The Superintendent let them finish, then took them through the points one by one. 'If Frank Leder and his wife didn't get on too well, was there anyone else—a steady girlfriend, say?'

Alan answered. 'No, no one steady, I'm sure. On the whole he was pretty faithful to Kathleen. It wasn't that he was specially unhappy with her. It was just—just that she was a pretty strait-laced woman.'

'I see,' said Thorne. 'And his drinking! Did he get depressed when he'd had too much?'

'No more than anyone else. In fact, he usually got aggressive. Not fighting drunk, but apt to be quarrelsome.'

'I see,' said Thorne again. 'Now, this question of money. Mr Poston, did you by any chance offer Mr Leder financial help with his business and then withdraw the offer?'

Alan looked across at his wife as if seeking advice. 'You mean, did I promise him something and then let him down?' he said, before Diana intervened.

'My husband has always been very generous to Frank Leder,' she said quietly. 'Over the years he's lent Frank a lot of money—and I may say we wouldn't dream of asking Kathleen to repay any of it now. But there was never any undertaking to take any part in his business, though I think he might have welcomed the idea.'

Thorne accepted this. He thanked them for answering his questions so frankly, apologized again for disturbing their afternoon and rose to take his leave. Celia showed the two detectives through the house to the front door.

'Poor Frank,' she said. 'To be honest, I didn't like him all that much. He could be very—irritating sometimes. But he and Alan were old friends, and he did save Alan's life once.'

'He did?' Thorne had been about to say goodbye, but he stopped in the doorway, interested. 'How was that?'

'Oh, it was ages ago. We were all in the south of France. Alan got into difficulties swimming. Normally he's a terrifically strong swimmer, but one morning he suddenly got cramp. He'd almost certainly have drowned if Frank hadn't realized what was happening and gone to the rescue.'

'Good for Mr Leder,' Thorne commented. He smiled at Celia; he rather liked her. 'Good afternoon to you, Miss Frint.'

★

'Well, Abbot,' Thorne said as they turned from the drive on to the road. 'If you can tear your mind from that shapely maiden for a minute, tell me what you thought of the Postons and their chums.'

'Maiden?' Abbot snorted. 'I bet she's no maiden, not living with that lot. What a ghastly crowd!'

'Made you sympathize with Mrs Leder, did it?'

'I'll say. That guy Dinsley not giving a damn what he showed! And the topless woman!'

Thorne grinned. 'Apart from that, did anything else strike you?'

Bill Abbot shook his head in bewilderment. 'I don't rightly know, sir. Except for the girl Celia Frint, they seemed—unnatural, somehow—almost as if they were acting parts, pretending to be very casual, but underneath all tensed up, if you know what I mean. Why should a visit from a couple of coppers throw them into such a state?'

'Heaven knows. Bad consciences, maybe.' Thorne was thoughtful.

'But it doesn't help much, does it, sir? I meant about Leder. I mean, suppose one of them could have got him to drink that cyanide, what would he—or she for that matter—have to gain? It's the Postons who've got all the money,—not Leder.'

Thorne nodded his agreement. 'And as for us,' he said sardonically, 'we may not have much money but we've got plenty of work ahead. We've no need to search for it.'

CHAPTER 17

Frank Leder was buried a week later. Superintendent Thorne did not attend. The inquest had been brief, the evidence minimal, the verdict predictable: '. . . while the balance of his mind was disturbed.' There were insufficient grounds, the police had concluded, to warrant their asking for an adjournment and, though the Superintendent remained somewhat unsatisfied, there was nothing more that he could do.

The funeral—held appropriately enough on an afternoon of grey skies and intermittent drizzle—was surprisingly well attended. Apart from Kathleen and a few relatives, the group from the lodge—Alan, Diana, Celia, Guy and Tony —were naturally present, together with a sprinkling of other friends and business acquaintances. The factory was closed for the day as a mark of respect and, since Leder had been well-liked by his staff, many of them came to the church. The congregation was completed by a large number of newsmen and photographers; the slightly bizarre aspects of suicide in an up-market toy factory, with the victim clutching at a stuffed unicorn in his death throes, had not escaped the editors of the tabloids.

Only the family had been asked back to the Leders' house and, since the weather was so unpleasant, Diana decided she and Alan, Guy, Tony and Celia would not take part in the final ceremony at the graveside, but would return at once to the manor. Diana had wasted no time over the move to the big house and they had all left the lodge two or three days ago.

Celia was far from sure that she liked the change. The lodge had always been the equivalent of a country cottage, where everything had been casual and informal. By contrast the manor seemed to her pretentious and unwelcoming, constantly reminding her of Sir Oliver and Tom Calindar and how much she missed them both. Her relationship with the Harmans had changed subtly but unmistakably. Though perfectly polite, the couple were less friendly than they had been in the past, and she no longer felt comfortable in the servants' quarters.

For that matter, Celia felt uncomfortable everywhere in

the house, except in her own bedroom. Here she could relax and be at ease. Elsewhere there was tension and irritation and tempers that flared at the slightest provocation. Celia was at a loss to understand the situation; surely, she thought, at least Diana and Alan should have been happier now that the manor was theirs, and money was no longer a problem.

It was just after three when they reached the house, and if the weather had been better, Celia might have gone for a walk or down to the pool for a swim. As it was, she roamed restlessly about her room, wishing she were back in Paris. The rain and the funeral had combined to depress her further. It was, she realized, the third funeral she had been to in less than a year.

Eventually, bored, she found her way downstairs. There was no one about and no sign of tea, so she went into the library in search of a book. There were few novels on the shelves, none of them modern, but she found a collection of short stories that looked interesting. Curling herself up in a big winged chair, she began to read.

Celia was one of those people with the ability to become totally absorbed in something she was reading. She failed to notice the library door opening and shutting, and she was unaware that anyone had entered the room until she heard voices. Even then only a part of her mind took in what was being said.

'I'm just about fed to the teeth. First we waited for old Oliver Poston to die. Then we waited interminably for his will to be probated. And now we're still waiting. What for? We had an agreement—a firm agreement.'

'Tony, you sound just like Frank Leder.'

'Too bad. Maybe he had a point. Some things aren't worth waiting for if the wait's too long.'

'Just what do you mean by that? Di?'

'No, damn it, I don't mean Di. I mean the money. All Di can think of at the moment is prancing round the manor making notes about the alterations and redecoration she's planning. If she wants to play the chatelaine, that's fine with me, Guy, but I need my share of the money now. And I want the whole business of Alan finished and done with.'

Celia had stopped reading now, and was unashamedly listening. She hadn't intended to eavesdrop, but by the time she realized that Guy and Tony were holding a private conversation it would have been embarrassing to interrupt. Besides, she could hardly fail to be intrigued by the content of their words.

'My dear chap,' Guy was saying. 'I couldn't agree with you more. The sooner we can get rid of Alan, the better, but—'

Celia's book slid off her lap and landed on the carpet with a thud. It was only a small noise, but it was enough to stop Guy in mid-sentence. He was across the room and standing over Celia before she could move. Momentarily his expression was stern, even fierce, and Celia was afraid. Then he relaxed, shook his head and grinned at her.

'It's okay, Tony,' he said. 'Only Celia, fast asleep over a book.' He winked at her.

Tony came to stand beside Guy. 'Young girls shouldn't go to sleep in the middle of the afternoon,' he said. It was difficult to tell from the tone of his voice if he believed what Guy had just said.

'It's such a beastly day, and I was bored,' Celia said.

'Bored? At your age?' Guy sounded mockingly avuncular.

Tony picked up the book and handed it to her. 'Anyway it's time for tea. I'm going to find Di.'

As he went ahead of them Guy drew Celia back. 'Haven't you ever heard that old saw that listeners never hear any good of themselves?' he asked casually.

'But you weren't talking about me,' Celia replied. And, as Guy laughed, she realized immediately that she had given herself away.

'So you did hear what we were talking about,' he said.

'Yes, I suppose so,' Celia admitted, 'but I didn't understand it.'

'Perhaps it's time you did, love,' Guy said. 'It's really very simple. Di wants to divorce Alan and marry Tony. Alan's agreed. He's quite happy about the arrangement and he's promised she should have the manor and a substantial amount of money. It's the money that's the problem. Oh, there's no shortage of it now—even that lawyer man Worth has to advance anything they need. But it's going to take time to sell bonds and shares and property and all the things it's tied up in—to make it liquid, as they say—so that it can be divided. In the meantime, I'm afraid poor old Tony's getting impatient.'

'I see,' Celia said slowly.

She had no reason to doubt Guy, but somehow his explanation didn't seem altogether to fit the conversation she had overheard, and she suspected there was a good deal he hadn't told her. Somewhat uneasily she followed him to the drawing-room, where they found Diana speaking heatedly to Alan and Tony. The colour was high on her cheeks and she was clearly very angry.

She turned to Guy and Celia. 'No tea today,' she said dramatically. 'Not unless we get it ourselves.'

'Well, that's not difficult. I'll do it,' Celia volunteered.

'Don't be silly! Of course it's not difficult, but that's not the point. I expect the Harmans to get tea. It's what they're paid for. Can you believe it, I found them lounging in their flat. They say it's their half day off.' Diana was still seething. 'Though why they couldn't tell us in advance, I'll never know.'

'Maybe you never asked them,' Tony said mildly.

'Why the hell—' began Diana.

Alan interrupted her. 'You mean there'll be no dinner tonight either?' he asked.

'But there must be plenty of food in the house,' Celia objected. 'We can cook it ourselves. We did at the lodge.'

Diana ignored Celia and sighed with exasperation. 'There'll be no dinner tonight or any other night until we find another couple. I told the Harmans they could get out. Right now. As soon as they can pack. They can have any money that's due to them in lieu of notice and damn well go. We'll send any heavy trunks after them.'

'Well, that's too bad, but if it's what you want—' Tony said. 'Mrs H is an absolutely splendid cook, though I must admit she's a nosy woman. Even at the lodge I got the impression she was keeping a weather eye on us and our doings.'

Guy laughed. 'It may have been a weather eye, but it was certainly a disapproving one.'

'That's true,' Tony agreed.

'Spying on us,' Diana said bitterly. 'That's what they were doing—both of them—spying on us. Personally I'm thankful to be rid of them, though they had their uses.'

'Like getting tea,' Celia said. 'Okay. I'm off to the kitchen. Let's hope Mrs Harmans's left us a cake.'

She was half way along the corridor when it occurred to her that, because of the funeral, they'd all had a very early lunch. Someone might perhaps like sandwiches or something more substantial. But there was no point in making the effort if the food wouldn't be eaten. She retraced her steps to inquire and reached the door of the drawing-room in time to hear Guy say, 'Well, it's a shame about poor old Frank, but it does mean there'll be that much more for each of us when old Alan coughs up.'

Silently, wishing she'd not returned, without waiting to hear what comment if any 'old Alan' might make, Celia retreated to the kitchen.

After tea the weather unexpectedly cleared. The rain stopped and a pale sun dispersed the clouds. As it grew stronger the earth steamed, while the trees continued to drip and sparklets of water shone on the grass. It became a hot and muggy evening—too hot and muggy, as everyone agreed, to think of changing and going out for a meal.

Eventually Tony suggested a swim, but no one showed any enthusiasm. Celia, having cleared away the tea-things, said that she was going for a walk. Diana said she would have to see what, if anything, the Harmans had left in the way of food, adding that she expected some help. Miming reluctance, Guy followed her to the kitchen. But Tony persisted with his suggestion, and finally he persuaded Alan to go with him.

Celia had no wish for company, and she was glad no one had volunteered to walk with her. She somehow felt she needed to think, though she was unsure about exactly what. Perhaps she should consider what Guy had told her, and try to relate it to the increasingly odd atmosphere she'd noticed, the tensions, her growing certainty that she was being excluded from some vital factor or facet of life among the Postons and their friends. She was no longer a child but she was suffering the same sense of disquiet, of apprehension almost, that she'd had when she was ten or twelve years old and she'd first caught out Diana or Guy in a barefaced lie. She couldn't remember the occasion or the details, but she recalled vividly what she now knew was a genuine sense of insecurity . . .

Her thoughts drifted to her own position. In three years' time she would inherit a hundred thousand pounds, and would no longer be dependent on Guy and Diana. Indeed, that pleasant solicitor James Worth had made it clear that there would be no problem if she needed funds in the meantime for some reasonable purpose, such as her education. She hadn't forgotten Tony's suggestion that she might try to win a place at Oxford.

She made a wide circle of the manor grounds, trudging through wet grass and climbing a gate to get out on to a country road. It was a route she had sometimes taken with Nelson, and she wondered idly why Alan hadn't bought another dog. She was hot and sticky when she reached the bottom of the drive. The idea of a swim was attractive, and there was probably no need to go up to the manor first; they had all left their swimming gear at the lodge, and if Tony was still here so that the house was open—

Celia's thoughts were interrupted by a loud shout, abruptly curtailed. She stopped in her stride. It had sounded like a cry for help and it had come from the direction of the pool. The cry came again, but now less loudly. Celia began to run.

She reached the side of the pool too late to do more than help Alan out of the water. He was choking and gasping for breath, and it was a minute before he could speak. By then Tony had also pulled himself out of the pool to stand on the grass, head bent, a hand over one of his eyes, his face screwed up with pain.

'What is it? What happened?' Celia demanded.

'He—he tried to drown me,' Alan gasped. 'The bastard grabbed my ankle and held me under.'

'Nonsense! Bloody nonsense!' Tony was angry. 'Don't listen to him, Celia.'

'You pulled me down, you know you did! I was swimming perfectly peacefully and you pulled me down and held me under.'

'Only for a second. I was just fooling.'

'Fooling, my foot! You were bloody well trying to drown me.'

'Nonsense,' Tony said again, more mildly. 'Why should I want to drown you, Alan? You panicked, that was the trouble. And you kicked me in the eye, what's more. God knows what you've done to it. It hurts like hell.'

'Good!' Alan snapped viciously.

Celia looked from one of them to the other in amazement. They sounded, she thought, like two small boys—'You did! I didn't!'—but they were grown men and they seemed in deadly earnest. Certainly Alan appeared to believe what he was saying and it was obvious that he'd swallowed a lot of water. He was still retching, vomiting a little on to the grass, and his chest was still heaving. If Tony had merely been fooling, as he claimed, it was a bit of foolery that had gone badly wrong.

None of it made sense. Alan was a much bigger man than Tony, and a fine swimmer into the bargain. If Tony had really pulled him under and tried to hold him down, he might well have kicked Tony in the eye in his efforts to free himself. But he should have been able to get free easily, and not emerge from the struggle in his present condition, half drowned. There was more to the incident than the men had seen fit to admit. Celia could only guess that it was all to do with Diana. In any case, it was stupid.

She said coldly, 'I suggest you both get dressed and go back to the manor. Tony can have his eye looked at, and a strong drink should settle both your nerves.' It was a surprisingly adult remark, and neither man answered, though each regarded her speculatively as she turned her back and left them.

Celia's own desire for a swim had quite gone. She kicked a loose stone before her as she walked up the drive, and she had nearly reached the manor when she saw a car coming towards her. She stepped on to the grass verge to let it pass. It was a taxi, laden with luggage, the Harmans in the back were almost obscured by various bags and packages. They were both sitting stolidly upright, and although they clearly could not avoid seeing Celia they made no attempt at a gesture of greeting or farewell. Celia stood and watched the cab depart with regret, wishing she had not been forced to part with the couple on these terms. Then a curve in the driveway hid them from view.

CHAPTER 18

'I'm going to London tomorrow.'

Alan threw out this remark casually as he stood up and went to refill his glass. They were all in the drawing-room, drinking before dinner. Diana had been explaining the need to replace the Harmans as soon as possible. Tony and Guy had been suggesting possible sources or agencies. Celia was sitting to one side, sipping her drink, and saying little. All of them except Celia looked up sharply and stared at Alan in surprise.

'I'm going to London tomorrow,' he repeated.

'Why?' Diana demanded at length.

'Why? To see a girlfriend. To have a good time. To get away from you lot for a bit. Do I need better reasons?'

'How nice for us!'

Tony spoke with considerable asperity. His right eye was half closed, the flesh around it swollen and darkening; by morning it would be all shades of the rainbow. Alan had kicked him very hard.

'I shall take the Jaguar,' Alan said calmly. 'I'll leave right after breakfast. Any objections?'

Diana regarded him coldly. She had of course heard about the incident at the pool, and had been prepared to accept Tony's version. She supposed this sudden decision of Alan's was some sort of childish reaction. He was becoming more and more difficult, she thought, more and more self-assertive. It was absurd, when everything they had wanted was at last within their grasp.

She said, 'May we ask when you're returning?'

'When it suits me.'

'There may be things from Worth—papers for you to sign.'

'So what? They'll have to wait.'

Diana opened her mouth to protest, but Celia intervened. 'Oh, for heaven's sake!' she said. 'Can't you stop quarrel-ling?'

Guy supported her. 'She's right. Stop arguing. What's all the fuss? Why the hell shouldn't old Alan have a few nights on the town? A couple of days isn't going to make any difference.' Alan was about to say something, but Guy went on, 'Who finished up in charge of dinner tonight? When are we going to eat?'

The subject of Alan's departure was closed, at least for the moment.

They drank steadily for another half-hour, and then had their meal, most of which Mrs Harman had prepared in advance. Celia cleared away and Guy filled the dishwasher. They had coffee outside on the lawn. Afterwards Diana and Tony went for a stroll together, Guy said there was a programme on television he intended to watch and Alan retired to his room. Left to herself, Celia decided to have an early night, and followed Alan upstairs.

The sleeping arrangements at the manor had sorted them-selves out quite naturally. Diana had spurned Sir Oliver's rather spartan furnishings and had left his suite to Alan, herself taking over the main guest room with Tony nomin-ally next door. Guy had a room across the same corridor, while Celia found herself at the other end of the house.

It was about five o'clock the next morning when some-thing wakened her with a start. Celia lay in bed, straining her ears to listen, to hear again whatever sounds had dis-turbed her. Outside it was already light and the birds were singing.

Then the noises were repeated—shuffling and bumping in the corridor outside her room. She was reminded very forcibly of the night of Alan's accident, but this time she made no effort to get out of bed and see what was happening.

She lay very still, and was suddenly surprised to find she was holding her breath.

There was a thud against her bedroom door, a dull thump as if someone had fallen against it rather than a request to enter. But the handle was turning, the door opening. Celia sat up at once, turned on her bedside lamp and reached for her robe.

'Oh, it's you,' she said. 'What do you want?'

Alan had stumbled into the room and was now leaning against the door, having shut it behind him. He was breathing heavily and seemed to have some difficulty standing upright. Celia assumed he was drunk. She looked at him in disgust. He hadn't bothered her since the pass he'd made on the night of Sir Oliver's funeral, but she remained wary of him. Now she jumped to the conclusion that he was invading her room for the obvious reason.

'Get out!' she said when he didn't speak. 'Get out at once, Alan! If you don't I'll scream blue murder, and God knows what'll happen then.'

'No, Celia. Please. Please don't.' Alan's voice was hoarse and placating. 'Please. I need your help. I'm ill.'

'Ill?' Celia was suspicious. 'What do you mean—ill? You've had too much to drink, that's all.'

'No, no! I mean it! I'm desperately ill. I've been poisoned. They've poisoned me. I know it.' Alan groaned. 'Diarrhoea. Violent vomiting. For hours. I can't go on like this, Celia. I'm getting weak—dehydrated. It'll kill me. Help me. Please.'

Celia, by now convinced that Alan really was ill, slid out of bed, wrapped her gown round her and found her slippers. 'Okay, Alan. You go back to your room and lie down. I'll call Di. She'll know what to do.'

'No! No! Don't do that!'

Celia was surprised at his vehemence, assuming that he hadn't wanted to seek Diana's assistance because he knew that Tony would be with her. 'Why not?' she said. 'What does it matter? I said I'll call Di. We must. It's an emergency.'

'I—I don't trust her—or Tony or Guy. None of them.'

'What on earth do you mean?'

'For Christ's sake, Celia, don't argue.' Alan was almost crying. 'Get Dr Band!'

'All right,' Celia said doubtfully.

'Quickly! Now! Hurry!'

Alan turned, bumping into the door which he just managed to pull open before stumbling into the corridor. His arms bound tightly round his stomach as if to stop himself falling apart, he staggered to the nearest bathroom. Celia followed him. He knelt in front of the lavatory, retching drily into the pan and whimpering. His face was white beneath its tan and beads of perspiration shone on his skin.

By now Celia was truly alarmed. Wishing she had never doubted Alan, she ran down the stairs to the hall and through to the servants' quarters where she knew there was a phone with a list of emergency numbers.

Dr Band answered on the second ring. He listened, grunted, murmured soothingly, 'I'll be there as soon as I can,' and gently put down the receiver.

Mary Band was stirring. 'What is it, Dick?'

'More trouble at the manor,' he said. 'That was Celia. Apparently Alan Poston's sick. Sounds like food poisoning or the usual summer tummy bug. Probably not serious, but the girl's obviously worried. I'll have to go.' He was already out of bed and pulling off his pyjamas.

'Damn the Postons,' Mary Band said uncharitably, glancing at the bedside clock. 'They only call you when it suits them. Otherwise you're not good enough. Off they go to Harley Street.'

'You're forgetting old Sir Oliver,' he said, 'and that wonderful Corot he left us.'

'It was no more than you deserve,' said his wife fondly.

There was no reply, and she wondered if her husband had

not heard her. He had gone into the adjoining bathroom, and when he came back he was ready to leave. He picked up his bag and bent over the bed and kissed her.

'I may deserve the Corot,' he said, 'but the fact that we have it makes me feel responsible for the family. I'd like to forget Alan Poston and his wife—and the curious crew they associate with—but somehow I can't. They keep on turning up in slightly unusual circumstances—and they worry me.'

At that time of the morning there was little traffic and the doctor drove fast, but by the time he reached the manor the household had been aroused. The front door of the house was ajar, and Diana was waiting for him in the hall, with Celia. It was odd, Band thought, that it was the girl and not the wife who explained the circumstances briefly, as he was led to the suite where he had so often attended old Sir Oliver.

Alan was lying on his bed. He was flat on his back and covered with a duvet. There was sweat on his brow, but from time to time he shivered. As Band came into the room he drew in a great breath, as if of relief, and visibly relaxed.

'Good morning, Mr Poston,' Band said pleasantly. 'How are you feeling now? Miss Frint tells me you've been having a bad time.'

Alan gave a pathetic attempt at a smile and tried to sit up. The effort had its effect on him. He muttered some incoherent apology, leapt out of bed and dashed for the bathroom. When he returned he was shivering, and the sweat was heavy on his brow.

Dr Band helped him back into bed. 'Let's have a look at you,' he said quietly. He turned to Diana and Celia, who were still waiting in the room. 'If you'll excuse us—'

By the time the two women had gone, Alan Poston had recovered slightly from his latest spasm. He seized Band by the arm. 'I've been poisoned, Doctor. You've got to believe me. I know I've been poisoned. It was ghastly. I really thought I'd had it. If it hadn't been for that girl Celia—I feel a bit better every time I'm sick, but—'

Words poured out of him as he described what he had suffered, what he was still suffering. He didn't actually accuse Tony Dinsley of trying to poison him, but he came very near to it. 'Doctor,' he said finally. 'I want you to promise me something. If I die there's got to be a proper post mortem. I don't want Dinsley—or anyone else—to get away with it. Promise me.'

Band freed himself gently and made no comment. Instead, he popped a thermometer in his patient's mouth, pulled back the duvet and commenced his examination. Finally he said, 'Mr Poston, you're not going to die, at least not on this occasion. It's possible you've caught some bug—there's a certain amount of summer flu going around—but it's much more likely you've eaten something tainted and it's upset you rather badly. However, I can see no reason to suppose it's serious, or that it won't clear up in a day or two—'

'Not serious? Just something a bit off?' Alan was practically incoherent with indignation. 'Look, you can ask Celia —I had exactly the same things to eat as everyone else, but I'm the only one to be taken ill. And terribly ill, for all you say, Doctor—I suppose I'd have to be poisoned and die like poor Frank Leder for you to think it serious?'

'Mr Poston—' Band explained that it only needed one single small bit of tainted meat or fish to give rise to these symptoms. There was nothing extraordinary about the fact that no one else had been ill.

'Now,' he said, 'I'll leave you a couple of prescriptions. Get them made up as soon as possible, but in the meantime I'll give you some of the drugs to start taking immediately. I keep a few with me for moments like this.' He smiled encouragingly at Alan Poston as he rummaged in his bag. 'Take two of each of these right now and then one of each every four hours. Eat lightly, if at all. Most important, drink lots of clear fluids. And rest in bed. With any luck, you should be fine in forty-eight hours or so. If you have any more trouble let me know.'

Diana was nowhere in evidence when he left Alan's bedroom, and it was Celia who showed him downstairs. 'You did right to call me,' he said, 'but it's not really serious. There's no need to worry.'

Celia turned to Band and gave him a long, steady glance from her blue eyes. 'I'm not worried,' she said. 'At least, not about Alan's illness, now you've seen him. But—but I sometimes think he's going crazy. For instance, did he tell you he believes he was deliberately poisoned? He did? But that's absurd. And this afternoon when he and Tony were fooling in the pool, he—'

She made light of the incident, but it was clear to Dick Band how much it had disturbed her. He said, 'Miss Frint, is there anything else? Has your brother-in-law seemed to behave strangely before this?'

Celia shrugged. 'It's hard to think of anything special—unless you count a stupid pass he made at me a few months ago when he was drunk.' She hesitated. By now they had reached the front door. 'But he's been a bit odd generally ever since that accident. Doctor, you don't think he can have done something to his brain when he fell, do you? He did give his head an awful bang and he had no attention till he got to London the next morning.'

'I very much doubt it,' Band said reassuringly. 'He was given a clean bill of health by his London doctors, wasn't he? Anyway, it's Mrs Poston's problem, not yours.' He grinned at her.

'Yes, I suppose that's true,' Celia said, but she didn't respond to Dick Band's smile. According to Guy, she thought, Alan's health was not going to be a concern of Diana's for much longer.

★

Alan spent the day in bed. His diarrhoea had gradually eased and he'd not been sick since Dr Band had left, but he felt incredibly weak. It was an effort to sit up and drink the Perrier water with which Celia kept him supplied. Most of the time he dozed.

Diana looked in on him twice and Guy once, but he pretended to be too sleepy to talk. Tony didn't appear. The only person he was glad to see was Celia. She drove into Colombury to collect his drugs and fetched and carried for him, and fulfilled his few requests. By late in the afternoon, he was feeling relatively improved and prepared to consider something to eat. After some hesitation he agreed to try a pot of tea, a boiled egg and a piece of toast, as long as they were prepared for him by Celia. She propped him up with pillows and, because he asked her, sat and watched as he ate.

For something to say, she remarked, 'I hope it wasn't important that you didn't get to London today.'

'London!' Alan stopped eating and stared at her. 'Christ! I'd forgotten all about it.'

'Does it matter?'

'Yes. It does.' Slowly Alan began to eat again, considering.

When he'd finished, he said, 'Look, Celia, if I gave you a nice present would you do something for me without telling Diana or anyone?' His smile was sly.

Celia regarded him with some dislike. 'I'm not a child, Alan. You don't have to bribe me with sweets. What do you want?'

'I—I want you to phone a London number—I'll give it you—and ask for a Miss Nancy Naury. Explain that I'm ill and that I won't be able to get to town for a few days. Tell her I'm sorry. Will you do that?'

'Without telling Diana or anyone?'

'Yes. It's—it's none of their business.'

'All right.'

It was with considerable reluctance that Celia agreed to

the request. She had no wish to get involved with Alan and his girlfriends, but in the circumstances it didn't seem a great deal for him to ask. He gave her the number and during the course of the evening, out of earshot of any of the others, she tried to phone three times. But there was never any answer.

CHAPTER 19

The next day was to be one of the hottest of that summer. After lunch Celia lay on a chaise-longue in the shade of a big oak tree in the garden of the manor, desultorily turning the pages of a magazine. Diana and Tony and Guy had gone to the pool but Celia, having swum in the morning, had had little hesitation in opting for temporary solitude. Alan was upstairs, lying on top of his bed in his pyjama trousers and watching cricket on television.

None of them saw or heard the white sports car that swung through the gates and sped up the drive to come to an abrupt halt before the front door, sending gravel flying. It was not a new car, but a beautifully kept MG hardtop— a very appropriate vehicle for Miss Nancy Naury, who climbed out, wearing slacks and a halter top in bright yellow. Her usual cheerful expression was missing, and she looked both worried and defiant.

She slipped a jacket over her brief top, mounted the steps and rang the doorbell firmly. There was absolutely no response, and this disconcerted her a little. She had expected the door to be opened by a butler, or at least by a uniformed maid. After all, Alan—her Henry—was now enormously rich. More tentatively she tried the bell again.

Even in the shade of the tree it was hot in the garden. Celia thought yearningly of a long cool drink tinkling with ice cubes. But no one was going to fetch it for her. She slid

off the chaise-longue and went across the lawn, to enter the
house just as Nancy was ringing the bell for the third and,
she had told herself, the last time. Wondering if it might be
Dr Band, Celia went to open the door.

'Good afternoon.' Nancy gave her wide smile. This was
obviously no maid. 'My name's Naury—Nancy Naury. I'm
looking for Mr Poston. Is he at home?'

'Mr Poston?' Celia repeated. She had returned to Paris
before the inquest on Tom Calindar and had thus never
seen Nancy before. But she recognized her name; this was
the girl she had tried to phone yesterday on Alan's behalf.
'Yes,' she said finally, 'he's here, but I'm—'

'I should like to see him, please.' Nancy spoke with
considerable determination.

'I'm not sure that's possible.' Celia was wary; she wished
Diana was around to cope with the situation.

'Why not?'

'He's been quite ill. Actually he's a lot better today, but
he's still unwell.'

'Ill? What's been the matter with him?'

Celia hesitated. She wasn't sure what business it was of
this Miss Naury's but Alan *had* tried to get in touch with
her. 'I think the doctor believes it was some form of food
poisoning,' she said at last.

'Food poisoning! My Henry! Bad enough to call a doctor?'
Nancy was horrified. 'Then of course I must see him. At
once. Where is he?' She didn't exactly push past Celia, but
she wasn't going to wait on ceremony, not if her Hen—By
now she was in the hall. 'Where is Henry?' she asked again.
'Please show me the way, Miss—Miss—'

'Frint,' Celia said. 'I'm Celia Frint. My sister's married
to Alan Poston. Alan.' She repeated the name. 'Why do you
call him Henry?'

'Because—because—I just call him that. It's a kind of
pet name.' Nancy looked at Celia in some exasperation.
'You wouldn't understand.'

'Wouldn't I?' Celia thought she understood only too well. 'If you'll wait in the drawing-room, Miss Naury,' she said with some formality. 'I'll go and ask Alan if he would like to see you.'

Nancy ignored the request. 'He'll want to see me,' she said positively, 'and I'd most certainly like to see him. I've not driven all the way down here from London for nothing. You just lead the way, Miss Frint.'

'Very well.' Celia still spoke formally, but she was beginning to accept the situation. She could see little point in arguing further; if Alan was unprepared for his visitor, it was too bad. 'Incidentally, Miss Naury,' she said as they walked upstairs together, 'Alan asked me to phone you yesterday to explain that he was ill, but there was no answer. I tried three times.'

Nancy nodded. 'It's that damned phone of mine. It's always going on the blink. God knows how many jobs I've missed because of it.' Then her voice softened. 'But the poor lamb! He didn't forget me, even when he was sick. You know, I was sure something was wrong when he didn't come yesterday. It was my birthday and he'd promised faithfully. He'd never stand me up without a good reason. That's why I came down here—to see.'

Celia could only smile at the obvious affection in Miss Naury's voice. They had reached Alan's door and she knocked sharply, but the television was loud and Alan was engrossed in the match. He had no warning before the door was flung open. His expression, Celia thought, as Nancy Naury ran towards the bed, arms wide to embrace him, was certainly not welcoming. Rather, it was a mixture of astonishment and horror, though Miss Naury didn't seem to notice.

'Hen! My darling Henry!' Nancy had flung herself on Alan and was kissing him violently. 'Thank God you're all right.'

Alan tried to push her away. 'Alan!' was the first thing

he said. 'Alan! I've told you before. My name's Alan. Don't call me Henry.'

But Nancy paid him no attention. 'You'll always be my Hen,' she said triumphantly.

Behind her back Alan gestured angrily at Celia and, grinning to herself, she departed, shutting the door firmly behind her. She went down to the kitchen and was starting to make herself a long lime drink when the telephone rang.

'Celia? It's me—Diana. Are you going to come down to the pool later?'

'I hadn't really thought. Why?'

'It's so hot we've decided to cut tea, and there's no white wine here at the lodge. We hoped you might bring us a couple of bottles when you come. Put them in the refrigerator now, there's a dear.'

'Yes, all right.' Celia paused fractionally. She didn't want to sneak on Alan, as it were, but Diana would be furious if she later heard about his visitor, and Celia hadn't mentioned her. If Diana hadn't phoned, Celia thought, she wouldn't have felt compelled to take any action, but as they were speaking there was really no alternative. She said, 'Di, do you know someone called Nancy Naury?'

'Yes, I've met her. Why?' Diana's voice was suddenly cold.

'She's just turned up in a super white sports car. She came to see Alan, though she calls him Hen or Henry. She said she was an old friend and it was a kind of pet name.' Celia did her best to sound bright and casual, as if it were commonplace for Alan's girlfriends to visit him unasked, complete with pet names. But she waited in some trepidation for Diana's reaction.

At first there was silence at the other end of the line. 'Di? Are you there, Di?' Celia said.

'I'm here. I was—thinking. This Miss Naury, she's with Alan now, is she?'

'Yes. She insisted and I—'

'That's okay, Celia. I understand. Forget about the wine, sweetie. I'll be along myself to collect it. Then I can have a word or two with Miss Naury. Don't let her go before I get there, will you?'

'All right. I'll try not,' replied Celia somewhat doubtfully; she was uncertain of her ability to make Miss Naury do anything she didn't want to. She put down the receiver and added aloud, 'Damnation!'

There was going to be a row, she thought, a stupendous row. Diana would come storming up to the manor with Guy and Tony and there'd be a dreadful slanging match before Miss Naury was finally shown the door. Deciding she would make herself scarce as soon as they arrived, Celia got some ice cubes for her lime juice and drank it slowly. She collected two bottles of Chablis from the cellar and put them in the refrigerator. Then she returned to the hall to wait.

The wait was longer than she had expected, and it seemed that she had misjudged Diana, for her half-sister arrived alone and showed no signs of anger. Celia relaxed; things might not be so bad after all. To confirm this hope, Diana had scarcely had time to enter the house before they heard Nancy Naury coming down the stairs. Diana went forward to greet her, hand outstretched.

'Good afternoon, Miss Naury. We've met before, if you remember. I'm Diana Poston.'

'Yes, I remember.' Nancy gave her wide, friendly smile, but it wasn't reflected in her eyes. 'When I was having a short break in the Cotswolds.'

'And you liked it so much you've come back again.'

'That's right. I happened to be passing, and I thought I'd call and see how Hen—er—Alan was doing.'

Diana didn't question this obviously false excuse. 'Of course, why not? You're one of his—friends, aren't you?' she said lightly. 'I notice you call him Henry. Poor Alan! In some ways he's very childish. Every time he gets a new girlfriend he seems to give himself a new name, just for her.'

Diana paused, and looked up sharply at Nancy as if expected her either to laugh in sympathy or attempt a contradiction. When Nancy made no obvious response, she continued, 'And poor Miss Naury too, perhaps. I regret to say that by now my husband's had a whole string of names, representing a whole string of girlfriends, though I expect he made out you were the only one he'd ever cared about.'

'No, Mrs Poston, you're wrong there. He told me no such thing. He wouldn't have been so stupid as to expect me to believe it.' Nancy drew herself up to her full height and looked down at Diana. In spite of the invidious position in which she found herself she was determined to remain cool. 'Now, if you'll excuse me, I think I'd better go.'

'Goodbye, Miss Naury,' Diana gave the visitor a long, speculative glance, then turned to Celia who had been standing in the background during this loaded conversation. 'Show Miss Naury out, will you, Celia.' With a brisk nod Diana departed into the drawing-room, leaving an embarrassed Celia to open the front door for Nancy Naury.

Outside, Nancy paused as if about to say something. Then she gave Celia a vague wave of her hand, ran down the steps and got into her car. For a moment she sat there. Though Celia couldn't see, she was trembling and her eyes were wet with tears, so that she had to grope for her key and only with difficulty managed to fit it into the ignition. She started the engine. Then, thankfully, she heard the front door shut and she got a handkerchief from her bag, wiped her eyes and blew her nose. She pulled down the sun visor and inspected herself in the vanity mirror concealed behind it. She had rarely felt more miserable.

Nothing had gone right. She had been so relieved when she discovered that her Henry hadn't let her down as she'd feared. He couldn't help being ill, and he'd tried to send her a message. There wasn't anything else he could do—except to welcome her when she arrived.

But he had not been in the least welcoming. On the contrary, when he had recovered from his initial surprise, he had been angry, very angry. He'd said she should never have come, she could only cause trouble, she must go before Diana learnt she was here.

Diana! That stuck-up bitch of a wife of his. Why didn't he leave her? Why didn't he divorce her? He wasn't in love with her—he'd admitted as much. And it couldn't be a question of money, not now. It was his money, after all, and there was so much of it. But he seemed almost—almost afraid of her. No—not exactly afraid. Committed to her, perhaps. Yes, that was the word—committed.

Nancy could only suppose that he was like so many other men, taking what was offered in the way of affairs, but safely tied to his wife, never intending to leave her. That was what Diana had implied, with her snide references to the succession of different names. And it could well be the truth.

Nancy Naury was a realist, and she faced the facts grimly. For her, Henry had become someone special, someone different from the others. She had to admit she was in love with the damned man. But that didn't mean he was in love with her. He had always seemed a little odd. Not in bed—she'd no complaints on that score—but in a variety of other small ways. She'd never felt herself able to depend on him, to trust him.

Telling herself that her best course would be to forget Henry—or Alan—she scrubbed her face with a handkerchief that was by now a sodden ball, jammed her foot on the accelerator and set off down the drive.

She passed the lodge, braking sharply as she came to the manor gates, and turned left on to the road; it was the way she had come and would lead her to the motorway and ultimately back to London. At least, that was her intention.

The road ran straight for a hundred yards or more. Then

there was an 'S' bend before it straightened once again. On one side a straggly hedge bounded the grounds of the manor. On the other a wood came within a few feet of the road surface, the large trees throwing long and confusing shadows in the late afternoon sunlight. There had been accidents at that spot before.

Nancy was a competent driver, rarely careless, though the road-holding capabilities of her sports car often encouraged her to drive too fast. And today she was upset and her mind wasn't fully on what she was doing. What was more, she had forgotten her seat-belt. Every factor was on the side of her would-be killer, though the decision to act had been taken quickly, even rashly.

Nevertheless, Nancy braked sharply as she came to the first bend of the 'S', and she went through the curves at a speed that was not unreasonable. Her mistake—a common one at this spot—was to try to accelerate out of the last bend too soon as the road stretched straight ahead of her, welcomingly bereft of traffic.

One moment the car was surging forward, and she was in control. The next, the hole appeared in the windscreen in front of the passenger's seat, and the world went white and blank before Nancy as the whole screen crazed. What she should have done was punch her fist through it at once, but this needed a split-second decision that she failed to take. And because she had been turning right and was not yet completely out of the bend, she continued to turn.

The little white car drove hard and straight into a tree. As the sound of crunching metal and shattering glass died away, Nancy Naury was left wrapped around her steering-wheel.

CHAPTER 20

As soon as she had shut the door behind Nancy, Celia turned to the drawing-room to look for Diana. Diana, however, was not to be found. Celia went back to the hall and called, without result. Shrugging, she returned to the kitchen. After those scenes, another long drink was attractive. When she opened the refrigerator she noticed that the bottles of wine were still there, so presumably Diana had gone up to Alan rather than back to the pool.

Slightly disgruntled, glass in hand, Celia returned to her chaise-longue beneath the oak tree. Here, her magazine ignored, she sipped her drink and thought of Nancy Naury. She had rather liked Miss Naury. Almost at once she heard a dull thud, then a muted crash. In the still summer air the sounds were loud enough to make her lift her head and listen, but when nothing else followed she dismissed them from her mind. She had no reason to connect them with Nancy.

In fact, Nancy Naury had been very, very lucky. She was unconscious and if her car had caught fire she would have had no hope of escape. If help had been long delayed—and even in summer this was not a highly frequented road—or if the help had been inadequate or inefficient, she would undoubtedly have died of her injuries. But, fortuitously, some few minutes after the crash a police patrol car, making for Colombury, came past.

The two uniformed officers wasted no time. They used their radio to summon an ambulance, and after a surprisingly short interval Nancy was on her way to Oxford with at least a chance of survival. Now events had turned in her favour, to the disadvantage of her would-be killer.

★

Sergeant Court put down the receiver as Dr Band came into
Colombury police station. 'That was Oxford, Doctor,' he
said. 'You know there was another accident yesterday at
that damnable S-bend on the Fairfield road, on the edge of
the Poston estate. The young woman who spiked herself
on the steering-wheel—they say they managed to operate
successfully, but her chances aren't great.'

'I did know there'd been a crash,' Band said. 'Too bad.'
He shook his head in commiseration. 'Who was she—a
local? I never heard.'

'No. Most of the locals treat that bit of road with respect.
She was a Londoner. A Miss Nancy Naury, apparently.
Something ought to be done—'

Dick Band stopped listening. He had heard Sergeant
Court before on the dangers of the Fairfield road. He was
remembering Nancy Naury. He had a good memory for
names and he was sure that he wasn't mistaken. She was
the tall thin girl with the wide smile and the white fake fur
who had sat next to him at Tom Calindar's inquest. He
recalled how she had greeted Alan Poston as an old friend,
and the Postons' peculiar reactions; he had been intrigued
at the time. Now Miss Naury had had an accident not far
from the entrance to the Postons' estate. It was almost
certainly coincidence, but—

He interupted the sergeant. 'How did it happen?'

'What? Oh, yesterday's accident. Usual thing, as far as
we can tell. She came round the last bend too fast and went
slap into a tree.' Court sighed. 'Probably confused by the
shadows, though we could be wrong. One of my men who
found her said there was a large round pebble and some
gravel on the floor of the car. If she'd been following a truck
or something and a wheel had thrown it up, it could have
shattered the windscreen. She might have been blinded
temporarily.'

'I see,' Band said noncommittally.

An unpleasant idea had occurred to him. He did his best to dismiss it, but throughout his day of house calls and surgery it hovered at the back of his mind, refusing to disappear. It was still there when he reached home that evening. Even then he would have been very reluctant to take any action, but he had hardly got inside his front door and been greeted by his wife when she remarked, 'Mrs Harman telephoned a short while ago, Dick. Something about you looking out for a job for them.'

'Yes. I promised I would—and I do have a possibility. It would be a great deal easier if they weren't so anxious to stay in the immediate neighbourhood, but—'

'It's become urgent for them, Dick. That Mrs Poston has kicked them out of the manor at a moment's notice and they need somewhere to live.'

'What?' Band stopped in the middle of pouring himself a whisky and soda. He was off duty till the next morning, and had been looking forward to a quiet, peaceful evening. Now, owing to Diana Poston, it seemed threatened with disruption. 'Why? Why should she have kicked them out?'

'You'd better ask the Harmans that,' Mary Band said. 'They're staying with Tom Calindar's sister in Fairfield for the moment. I wrote the number down on your pad.'

'Thanks!' Dick Band's reply was a little ironic. 'I think you're right—I'd better.'

His wife looked after him curiously as he went into his study, taking his drink with him. He dialled Beth Horton's number, and exchanged niceties with her till Mrs Harman came on the line. She explained that her husband was out, but she was fully prepared to expatiate on her grievances.

'—and there we were,' she said finally. 'Turned out, told to leave at once, and not a thought given as to where we were to go. It's not the money, Doctor. Sir Oliver was generous, as you know. It's the inconvenience and—and—Harman and me—we're not used to that sort of treatment.

It amounts to being dismissed without a reference of any kind, as far as we can see.'

'I understand your point, Mrs Harman,' Band said soothingly. 'And you say this was all because you didn't warn Mrs Poston that it was your half day off.'

'That was the—the excuse she made.'

'You mean you think there was some other reason?' Against his better judgement Band pursued the implication.

'Yes, Doctor, I do.' Mrs Harman lowered her voice so that Band had to press the receiver to his ear. 'I think the real reason was that I saw a rather—rather shaming scene the other day. It was a wet, miserable afternoon and they all came traipsing over from the lodge. Mrs Poston was determined to show them round the manor. And she did. They were pulling dust-covers off and fingering everything. I followed them around. I felt sort of—responsible.'

'Yes, or course. That was quite reasonable.' Band tried to sound as encouraging as possible while Mrs Harman paused for breath.

She went on to explain how arguments had arisen among the visitors, as she called them—arguments about who really owned the manor now, about old Sir Oliver's money. None of it had made much sense to her. 'Even that Mr Leder who poisoned himself seemed to think he was entitled to a share,' she said. 'But they were all so angry it was hard to follow what they were saying—Mrs Poston especially. In the end, she even went so far as to smack Mr Alan across the face. It's not the sort of behaviour you expect, is it, Doctor?'

'No indeed,' Band agreed evenly.

That seemed to be the end of Mrs Harman's story, and Dick Band told her of the post he hoped might suit her and her husband. She thanked him and he said goodbye. He went back to his sitting-room thoughtfully. Usually he confined himself to one whisky before dinner, but tonight he poured himself a second drink—and a strong one—and sat in silence, staring at the Corot he had inherited from Sir Oliver, until his wife became exasperated.

'For heaven's sake, Dick,' she said at last with some asperity. 'What's the matter now? You can't be that worried about the Harmans, so it must be the Postons again. You're obsessed with that wretched family.'

'Maybe, Mary, but I just feel there's something wrong there, terribly wrong."

'It's none of your business, Dick. You've had it out with Superintendent Thorne and he's told you there's nothing he can do.'

'He also told me he'd be interested in any developments —in anything else I thought relevant.'

'Then you'd better get on the phone to him right away,' Mary Band said decisively. 'At least it'll stop you mooning about like a sick duck. Dinner won't be ready for half an hour so you've plenty of time. But, Dick, promise me. If Thorne says again that nothing can be done you'll forget the whole thing.'

'I'll try,' said Dr Band.

In fact, Dick Band's promise to his wife was unnecessary. Thorne appeared to take what the doctor had to say with the greatest seriousness, and assured him that at the first opportunity he would look into the matter. Band, relieved that the Superintendent hadn't thought him importunate, returned in triumph to report to his wife.

The opportunity Thorne was seeking arose the very next day. Another senior officer returned from sick leave earlier than had been expected, and was able to relieve the Superintendent of the extra duties he had been forced to shoulder. At least in theory, he now had a little spare time.

His first step was to phone the Oxford hospital. He was told that Miss Naury's condition was stable, but she was still in intensive care and the prognosis was not particularly hopeful. It was quite impossible that he could interview her. He asked if she had made any comment on the accident, and was informed that she had scarcely spoken. She had muttered what sounded like the name 'Henry' a couple of times, but that was all. The hospital had naturally telephoned the number they had found in the patient's bag, which appeared to be that of her home in London, but had received no reply. They had no idea who this 'Henry' might be.

So far, so good, thought the Superintendent. At least Nancy Naury was being well cared for, and was perfectly safe for the moment. He warned Sergeant Court, collected Abbot and set off for Colombury. Court was more than a little surprised by the Superintendent's interest, but he at once made available the local uniformed officers who had been first on the scene of the accident. Together the four of them inspected Nancy's white car, now a write-off awaiting disposal in a yard behind a Colombury garage. Thorne gave instructions that it should receive a detailed technical examination, and he and Abbot were shown the stone and gravel found inside it.

Their next move was to the Fairfield road itself. They set off in two cars and drew up some fifty yards beyond the fatal S-bend. 'It really is a black spot, as Sergeant Court told you, sir,' one of the local officers said, as they assembled beside the road. 'There've been several bad accidents here over the years.'

Thorne strolled back, so that he could walk around the bends, the way that Nancy had driven. He walked slowly, and when he came to the beginning of the straight he stopped and looked from side to side with care. Then, measuring distances with his eye, he moved backwards even more slowly along the verge between the road surface and the hedge, opposite the trees.

At one point he pushed through the hedge into a field. He asked who owned the land, and was told it was probably part of the Postons' property. The grass here was short and showed no signs, but a yard or two from where he stood there was a small heap of gravel with a few larger stones in it—probably a relic of some past road work. Thorne picked up one of the stones and stood, half in and half out of the hedge, facing towards the bend.

It was possible, he thought. The angle was right. The risk of being seen by the driver of the car was negligible, especially among dappled shadows. In any case, Nancy Naury would have had her eyes on the road and, even if she had noticed some movement by the hedge, it would have been too late for her to react. But no one would have hurried down here on the off chance of finding a suitable projectile in just the right location as Nancy's car approached. If it were murder—or attempted murder—it had been premeditated.

Thorne stepped back on to the road, to join Abbot and the two local officers, who had been watching him with considerable interest. He showed them the stone he had picked up.

'It's a bit like the one in the car, isn't it?' he said. 'And I found it in a heap of gravel.'

One of the local officers was quick to comment. 'It's a bit large to have been thrown up by anything except a heavy truck—and we don't get many of those on this road,' he said. 'It could happen, though. But more likely some kid walking along just chucked it at the windscreen. Is that what you're thinking, sir?'

'Something like that,' Thorne agreed. He said they had seen all they wanted, thanked the two local officers and dismissed them. Then, with Abbot, he turned towards his own car.

'Where to, sir?' asked Abbot.

'The so-called manor,' Thorne said at once. 'I think a call on the Postons is in order.'

★

The front door was opened by a man in a white coat and dark trousers, who regarded them superciliously. Thorne had never seen him before, but assumed he was a replacement for Harman.

'Detective-Superintendent Thorne and Detective-Sergeant Abbot. To see Mr Poston,' Thorne said shortly.

'He's expecting you—sir?'

Thorne didn't like insolence. 'Just tell him we're here,' he said abruptly.

The houseman left them in the hall and disappeared. Five minutes later, when Thorne's patience had almost come to an end, Alan Poston arrived, accompanied by his wife. Poston, Thorne thought, was looking haggard and ill, eyeing them warily as Diana greeted them in her usual brittle manner and led the way into the drawing-room. At first she didn't ask them to sit down and the four of them stood in the middle of the room in an awkward group.

'Now, what's all this about, Superintendent?' Diana said. 'More of your questions?'

'Unfortunately, yes, Mrs Poston.'

'So what is it this time? Surely you're not still worrying about Frank Leder's death, are you?'

'On this occasion I'm concerned about another of your friends,' Thorne said blandly. 'A Miss Nancy Naury.'

'An acquaintance rather than a friend,' Diana said immediately.

'But she was visiting you on the day of her accident. In fact the accident happened as she was leaving here.' He made it a statement, and added. 'You did know she had a dreadful car crash?'

'Yes,' said Diana.

Alan Poston cleared his throat. 'How—how is she?'

Thorne shrugged. 'I suppose there's hope. But she was very seriously hurt.'

Poston nodded and turned his back, walking over to the windows. He stared out at the garden as if he were no longer

interested. Diana's smile was thin, but at last she sat down
and gestured to Thorne and Abbot to find themselves chairs.
She didn't speak, but merely looked inquiringly at the
Superintendent.

Thorne said, 'Mrs Poston, perhaps you or your husband
would be good enough to tell us about Miss Naury's visit.'

'Certainly.' Diana crossed her legs and smoothed down
her skirt. 'Though I can't see what it has to do with her
accident. My husband was in bed, recovering from an attack
of food poisoning—' Her account was brief and seemingly
factual.

'So her visit was completely unexpected?' Thorne said.

'Why, yes,' Diana agreed. 'And rather unfortunate. As I
said, I wasn't even here, and my husband, who was far from
well, wasn't very welcoming. Celia should never have taken
Miss Naury up to him. Anyway, I regret to say she left in
something of a huff.'

'You saw her out yourself?'

Diana frowned as if the question puzzled her. 'Since you
ask, no. I said goodbye and went back to the pool. Celia
saw Miss Naury out to her car.'

Thorne knew there were other questions he could ask,
but he was on slippery ground and didn't want to show his
hand or press too hard. He got to his feet and signalled to
Abbot. Alan Poston had turned away from the windows,
and the Superintendent was thanking both of them for their
cooperation when Celia came into the room.

'The Superintendent's been asking us about Nancy
Naury,' Diana said quickly.

'But I needn't bother you any more,' Thorne said, smiling
at Celia. He moved towards the door. 'Incidentally, do you
know anyone called Henry?'

There was a moment's silence that was almost palpable.
Then Diana said, 'Henry's a very common name.' But
Celia's face had given her away as instinctively she looked
at Alan. Alan stood quite still, wetting his lips.

CHAPTER 21

The Superintendent found himself occupied with other duties for the rest of the day, but Abbot with the help of his own notes and those Thorne had made after his talks with Dr Band, was set to work compiling a report on the Poston case—if it was a case. It was all good practice for the Sergeant, as Thorne pointed out, adding that he would appreciate Abbot's views.

The Superintendent's usual routine was to deliver his own views and demand questions, and Sergeant Abbot considered this somewhat unaccustomed request for assistance a challenge. He worked hard and, as Thorne was about to leave the office that evening, produced a file which he had labelled, 'The Poston Affair'.

'Sounds like a thriller,' Thorne grunted. 'Should make good bedtime reading. I'll take it with me. Maybe it'll help me to sleep.' Sergeant Abbot regarded his superior suspiciously, but Thorne's expression was bland.

In fact, while his wife Miranda cleared away the supper dishes and made coffee, George Thorne took the file into their garden. He read Abbot's report through, first rapidly, then more slowly. He was soon completely absorbed. He drank his coffee absently when Miranda held the cup out to him, but even his favourite chocolate mints remained untouched on the table beside him.

Miranda Thorne was an attractive woman, plump but not fat, with curly brown hair and clear brown eyes. What was more, she was highly intelligent, and she had been married to her husband for sixteen years. She knew better than to interrupt him on such an occasion. They were a devoted couple, though some of her friends pitied Miranda for her apparently dull existence as a childless housewife. What they didn't know was that she led another life as a respected compiler of crosswords and acrostics for newspapers and magazines. 'It's a bit like some of my work,' George was accustomed to remark, as he discussed his cases with her and in his turn made suggestions for her puzzles.

Now, she removed the coffee tray and returned to her needlework. She sat in the late evening sunshine, knitting placidly. Her product was to be a bright yellow sweater for her husband.

Thorne was impressed by the structure Abbot had attempted to build with so few bricks and so little mortar to hold them together. The sergeant had started from the most likely of the many possible crimes in the chain of events, and assumed that Tom Calindar had been murdered. A motive for this was hard to suggest—unless Sir Oliver had also been killed, and Calindar had found grounds to suspect the villain. Leder's death—and in spite of the verdict of the inquest it remained reasonably possible that this too was the result of criminal action—would suggest that he might also have been implicated, probably financially. From all this Abbot had proceded to build up a case against Alan Poston, who obviously had a lot to gain from his father's death.

But the situation was more complicated than that. Alan had made no secret of his fear that Dinsley wanted to kill him—either by drowning him or poisoning him. Perhaps Alan had faked both episodes, though this seemed highly unlikely. The alternative—probably even less likely—was some kind of conspiracy, presumably involving Diana, who would certain now benefit from her husband's death. But how did Nancy Naury fit in? Accident? Or had she also come to know too much?

It was all guesswork, Thorne thought ruefully, all theory. There were so many imponderables, so many unanswered questions, so little hard evidence. There was no doubt the whole set-up stank, but there was no obvious pattern to it. Thorne sighed heavily and shut the file.

'Want to talk?' asked Miranda.

Thorne grinned and relaxed. He helped himself to a mint. He had already told his wife a good deal about the Postons, and she listened, intrigued, as he filled in the rest of the story as he knew it.

'Any bright ideas?' he said when he had finished. 'Anything strike you?'

'Well,' Miranda spoke with some hesitation. 'There's this man Henry, whom Nancy keeps asking for. I've got a feeling he could be important—particularly so if you're right and the Postons were lying when they denied all knowledge of him. Why don't you ask that solicitor, Worth, if he's ever heard of a Henry in connection with the Poston family?'

'Yes. That's an idea. I suppose it's even possible that a Henry appears in Sir Oliver's will. Band never mentioned one, but he didn't necessarily give me all the details, and anyway he might have been so overwhelmed at inheriting his picture that he didn't notice.' Thorne stroked his moustache reflectively. 'But it's high time this business was made official. I can't go tackling solicitors or making any more inquiries without the Chief Constable's approval. Probably I've already gone further than I should without permission from on high.'

Miranda Thorne laughed, 'There wouldn't be anything new in that, George,' she said. 'See the Chief in the morning.'

The Chief Constable was a large and lazy-looking man, with a quick and sensible mind. He was prepared to overlook moderately unorthodox behaviour if it produced results, and he had considerable respect for the abilities and intuition of Detective-Superintendent Thorne. The Superintendent very often *did* produce unexpected results. So the Chief was ready to listen sympathetically to Thorne's exposition.

When Thorne had finished, the Chief made an immediate

decision. 'Right, Superintendent. Go ahead, but keep me in touch. You know as well as I do that we can't spare the time or the men for a long inquiry on such thin grounds, so you'll have to come up with something pretty soon—'

'I understand, sir. Thank you, sir.'

Thorne made his escape before the Chief was able to name an explicit deadline. First thing that morning, even before seeing the Chief, he had phoned the Met at Scotland Yard and asked them to get a copy of Sir Oliver Poston's will—now of course probated and thus readily available—and send it down to him on the facsimile link. He found Abbot putting the result on his desk as he returned to his room.

'Not wildly interesting, I'm afraid sir,' Bill Abbot said regretfully. 'The only Henry is old Sir Oliver himself. He was Oliver Henry.'

'And Alan?'

'He appears as Alan Richard. The old man apparently didn't pass on either of his names.'

Thorne grunted and started to read the will. As Abbot had said, it was disappointing and unhelpful, containing nothing important he didn't know already, nor any mention of a Henry. He asked for a call to be put through to James Worth.

Eventually, after Worth's office had been persuaded to phone back to confirm that his caller was really Detective-Superintendent Thorne of the Thames Valley Police, the solicitor seemed prepared to talk. 'What can I do for you, Superintendent? Something connected with the late Sir Oliver Poston, I gather.'

'Possibly, sir.' Thorne did his best to sound apologetic. 'In fact, we're trying to trace someone called Henry. We don't know his surname, and we appreciate there are millions of Henrys around, but we've reason to think this one may have been known to Sir Oliver. I've inquired from Mr Alan Poston, but he—er—couldn't help me.'

'You mean "wouldn't", Superintendent. Your voice gives you away.' There was a sound on the line which Thorne took to be a dry laugh. 'I admit that Mr Poston's not always the most helpful of men. Though in this case—' Worth paused, and Thorne waited hopefully, only to be disappointed when the lawyer continued. 'In this case he probably couldn't have helped you, even if he'd wanted to. At least that's true if the man you're speaking of is Henry Logan.'

'Henry Logan?' Thorne savoured the name. 'I don't know, sir. Perhaps he could be. Who's this Henry Logan?'

'Have you heard of Irene Cassington?'

'Yes. I've just read a copy of Sir Oliver's will. She was his secretary and his mistress, seemingly. He left her some thousands of pounds.'

'That's right, Superintendent. We had some difficulty in tracing her. She married an army man and they moved around a good deal. He—her husband—was killed in an accident during manoeuvres and she married again. Her second marriage is probably quite irrelevant to your inquiries, but her first husband was a Major Peter Logan. They had a son called Henry.'

'I see.' Thorne said slowly. He wished this interview were taking place face to face, so that he could watch the lawyer's reactions. 'Mr Worth, are you suggesting there's some possibility that—'

Worth interrupted him. 'I know what's in your mind, Superintendent. All I can tell you is that if Henry Logan was Sir Oliver's natural child, Sir Oliver knew nothing about it. Otherwise I'm sure he'd have taken steps to make some provision for the boy—probably over the years and certainly in his will.'

'I see your point, sir. Do you have an address for Henry Logan?'

'No, we don't. We were told he'd gone abroad—Australia, I think—but we weren't really interested. What we learnt about him was only incidental to our effort to trace his mother. We were able to establish that she died a few years ago, predeceasing Sir Oliver. You will have noted that in these circumstances under the terms of the will the bequest to her does not pass to any child of hers, but becomes part of the residual estate. That's why we weren't concerned with Henry.' Worth sounded surprisingly human as he concluded his explanation.

'And that's all you can tell me, sir,' said Thorne encouragingly.

'I'm afraid so, but I can let you have a note of the inquiries we made for Henry's mother—places and people and so on. You might get some help from that.'

Thorne was profuse in his thanks. He was well aware that it could be pure coincidence. Sir Oliver Poston's former mistress could have named her child Henry because it was her husband's second name, for instance. But, with no other leads, Henry Logan was certainly worth following up.

It was after lunch when Sergeant Abbot appeared in Thorne's office. A broad smile wreathed his pleasant face. Thorne, who had finally been forced to wrestle with some statistics for a long-overdue report, looked up hopefully.

'Henry Logan?' he guessed, expecting to anticipate Abbot.

Abbot shook his head. 'No, sir. Not yet. Miss Saint.'

'Who the hell—' Thorne began.

'The girl Nancy Naury shares a flat with, sir. Her name is Joy Saint. The Met have been trying to trace her, but she was away on holiday. Just returned from Spain this morning, and horrified to hear about Nancy. It seems Nancy's parents emigrated some years ago and she's no close relations in the UK, but this Miss Saint is the next best thing. Anyway, she's driving down to Oxford right away, and we've arranged for her to come here to see you when she's through at the hospital.'

'Splendid!' Thorne said, and returned to his figures. But as the afternoon progressed he found it more and more difficult to keep his mind on what he was doing. He was thankful when Abbot at last announced Miss Saint's arrival.

Miss Saint turned out to be something of a surprise to the Superintendent. Subconsciously he had been expecting a girl not unlike Nancy Naury. Joy Saint, however, was middle-aged and today, as she was ushered into his office with her heavy make-up stained with tears, she could easily have been fifty. There was something familiar about her which puzzled Thorne, though she explained as soon as she was seated.

'We've not met before, have we, Miss Saint?' Thorne said tentatively.

'Oh no. It's not that. I guess you recognize me from TV. It's astonishing how people do. I'm no star, but I appear often enough in bit parts and character parts. It all pays quite well. But you don't want to hear about me, Superintendent. It's my poor Nancy, isn't it?'

'I'm afraid so,' said Thorne.

In spite of her woebegone appearance Miss Saint was quite calm, and she told what she knew about her flat-mate clearly and concisely. Thorne let her talk until she ran out of steam. It was clear that she was very fond of the younger woman and had been appalled by the accident. The tears she blinked away through her mascara were genuine.

'What I don't understand,' she said at length, 'is why the police are so interested. Nancy didn't hurt anyone but herself, and God knows she's paying for it. Anyway, I don't believe detective-superintendents concern themselves with traffic matters.'

The Superintendent paused before replying. Then he said, 'Miss Saint, it's possible—and I stress the word "possible" —that someone deliberately threw stone and gravel at the car's windscreen. It blinded Miss Naury and caused the accident.'

'Some lout, you mean? For the hell of it?' Joy Saint radiated fury. 'Just let me get my hands on him.' But she still looked puzzled. 'Even so—a detective-superintendent. I've been in enough thrillers to know—'

Thorne interrupted her. 'Let's leave it, shall we, Miss Saint,' he said quietly. 'It's just a possibility, that's all. We're not sure, but we're looking into it. Anyway, that's not my primary reason for wanting to talk to you. Miss Naury has been asking for someone she calls "Hen" or "Henry", and we hoped you might help us to find him.'

'They asked me that at the hospital, and I didn't quite know what to say. But the police are different, I suppose.' She hesitated as Thorne looked up expectantly.

'Well,' Miss Saint went on, 'there shouldn't be any problem about finding Henry—not unless he's done another disappearing act—but there are complications—'

'Perhaps you'd explain, Miss Saint. Who's this Henry?'

'Nancy's boyfriend—sort of. Henry Logan.'

'Ah!' Thorne said involuntarily, and hurriedly turned the exclamation into a cough to hide his quickened interest.

'They're old friends, are they?' he prompted.

According to Joy Saint, Nancy had met Henry the previous summer in circumstances that could be called romantic. During a storm, when Nancy was unable to get a taxi and was making her way on foot to an important modelling engagement, her umbrella had turned inside out, and Henry had come to the rescue. Just like *Singing in the Rain*, they'd said. Henry seemed to be a gentleman, attractive and a nice chap, though he was a bit down on his luck at the time. Anyway, to cut a long story short, Nancy had fallen for him completely and in the end he'd moved into the flat with them.

'So?' said the Superintendent.

'Well, one morning, very early, long before any of us were awake, the phone rang. I got up and answered it myself. It was a woman wanting Henry. Henry told us it was his

mother, but I didn't really believe him, and I don't think
Nancy did either. Anyway, as soon as it got light he packed
a suitcase and left the flat there and then. He swore he'd
keep in touch, but of course he never did. Nancy felt dreadful
about it for a while, but she was beginning to get over him
when one day she saw his picture in one of those glossy
magazines. There was no doubt it was Henry, but according
to the magazine his name was Alan Poston and his father,
who'd just died, had been a very rich man.'

This time George Thorne found it impossible to hide his
surprise. But Abbot had dropped his pad on the floor, and
while he scrambled to pick it up Miss Saint stopped talking,
giving the Superintendent a moment to compose himself.

'Miss Saint,' he said, 'are you saying that Alan Poston
was masquerading as Henry Logan all the time Miss Naury
knew him?'

'Yes. He admitted it—'

'Admitted it? I thought you said he never got in touch
again.'

'He didn't get in touch with Nancy. It was Nancy who
got in touch with him. She went down to Colombury to—
to sort of spy out the land. I tried to persuade her not to,
but she insisted. I'm not exactly sure what happened, but
she saw Henry, though he was with his wife and didn't want
to know her. She was dreadfully upset when she got back
to London. However, a day or two later he phoned, and
they've been seeing each other ever since, whenever he can
get away from his wife.' She gazed at the Superintendent.
'It's not that unusual, you know.'

'I suppose not,' said Thorne. 'But what about the false
name?'

'Surely that was obvious. He hadn't wanted to tell Nancy
who he really was because he was married and sometimes
his name appeared in gossip columns. He said Henry Logan
was the first name that came into his head. And that,
Superintendent, is all I can tell you, I think. But I've got a

question. If Nancy wants her Henry she ought to have him. Shall I tell the hospital where to get in touch with him?'

Thorne regarded Joy Saint speculatively. 'I'd be grateful if you didn't,' he said finally. 'Earlier you mentioned complications. Well, let's say we've got some too. Let's keep it to ourselves, for the moment anyway. And before you go I've got one more question for you, Miss Saint. Would you know what day it was that Poston—Henry Logan—left your flat so suddenly?'

'As a matter of fact, I would. It was August the tenth— last year, of course.' Miss Saint smiled. 'No. You needn't be surprised. I don't have such a wonderful memory, but I do remember that date because during the afternoon I was offered a part in the West End—in a Coward revival. I'd specially wanted it; it suited me down to the ground.'

Thorne thanked her for her help, and Abbot showed her out. 'She has to be back in London next week,' the sergeant said on his return. 'Meantime she's staying in Oxford to be near Miss Naury and we can get her at the Randolph.'

'Good,' Thorne said absently, but Abbot doubted if he'd taken in his words. The Superintendent was busy going through the file on the Poston affair yet again. In fact, he was hoping that Henry Logan would prove to be more than a mere *nom-de-geurre* that Alan Poston had assumed to conceal his bit on the side. *Nom-de-guerre*, he thought: it could conceivably be a damned appropriate expression.

CHAPTER 22

It was later than usual before a satisfied Superintendent Thorne got into his car and headed for home. Though he was not yet sure of the identity of the killer, he at least had a working hypothesis which explained a good deal of what he had learnt and left only a few gaps. He intended to put his argument to his wife. If Miranda could find no great holes in it—and he was pretty sure it was watertight—he would start to check it out in the morning.

The initial checking shouldn't prove too difficult, though it would have to be done quietly, so as not to give the villain —whoever he or she might be—any warning. But once he'd decided on action, Thorne thought, speed would be important. There was no doubt that the killer was cunning and ruthless, and was prepared to take risks when the chips were down.

When it was possible, George Thorne liked to eat his meals in peace, and at home he usually made a point of not discussing his work over the table. But tonight was an exception. It was after nine by the time he was tackling the excellent supper Miranda had cooked for him, and he could wait no longer to give her a brief sketch of what he had discovered that day about the Poston clan.

When he had finished his exposition, his wife said, 'Perhaps you could get Dick Band now, George. Why don't you try? It would be nice to have some of the checking done tonight, wouldn't it?'

Thorne admitted that she was reading his thoughts, and went to the phone. He apologized for disturbing the doctor, and said, 'What I want is to get you to answer a few questions; some of them may see a bit inconsequential.'

'On our favourite topic?'

'Yes. Sorry.' Thorne's mind had been so occupied with the Postons that he had assumed Band would automatically know what he was talking about. He told himself to concentrate. 'The first thing to think of,' he said, 'is August of last year. Around the tenth. Did anything unusual happen then?'

'That's about when Alan Poston had his accident,' Band said at once. 'I'm surprised you don't remember.'

'I didn't want to prompt you,' Thorne said. 'Can you give me the exact date?'

There was a pause while the doctor went to find his last

year's appointments book. 'It must have been on the night of the ninth to the tenth that Alan cracked his head, or whatever he did. I didn't treat him, but I can date it from the eleventh, the Sunday when that dog Nelson took a bite out of Tony Dinsley.'

The night of the phone call, the night before Henry Logan left Nancy Naury's London flat so suddenly, Thorne thought triumphantly. 'Now, when did you next see Poston?' he asked.

'Next see Alan Poston? It was a week or ten days later, I think. I'd been visiting Sir Oliver and Alan and Diana drove up as I was leaving. He looked ghastly with his head bandaged.'

'And before then?' Thorne went on. 'When had you last seen him before then?'

Dick Band hesitated. 'You know, I can't have set eyes on him for a couple of years. I told you before that only Sir Oliver was a patient of mine.'

'And you never came across him when you were calling on Sir Oliver? Did he visit his father frequently?'

'No, very infrequently in fact. The old man used to complain about his neglect.' Band sounded puzzled. 'Superintendent, we've already been over a lot of this when we talked about the Postons. What's new now?'

Thorne didn't answer directly. He couldn't explain on the phone, so he contented himself with saying, 'I'm not really sure myself. But I'll be in touch. Many thanks for your help.'

He hung up before the doctor could ask more questions, and went into the kitchen where Miranda was laying the tray for their early-morning tea. 'So far, so good,' he said. 'It fits. Or, rather, it doesn't fit. If Alan was having a serious accident in Oxfordshire, how could he be in Nancy Naury's bed in London? And if he was a splendid swimmer before the accident, why was he such an indifferent swimmer afterwards? Why did he suddenly make a pass at Celia? And why did he want his beloved dog put down?' George Thorne stopped suddenly and gazed at his wife. 'Oh, what the hell?' he said. 'You know as well as I do there's only one sensible answer. Up till the accident Alan was Alan. After the accident—if it was an accident—Henry Logan became Alan.'

'Why?' Miranda asked gently.

'I guess because if Alan predeceased his father—and it's a fair bet he did—none of Sir Oliver's money would come to Diana. It would all go to charity—and I mean *all*, including the flat in London and the lodge, not to speak of the manor. Alan lived on his father's generosity. He had very little money of his own—not enough to satisfy Diana.'

'Alan and Henry must have been very much alike,' Miranda said thoughtfully. 'You say they were half-brothers, but—George, would such an impersonation really have been possible?' She took off her apron, hung it up and sat down at the kitchen table opposite her husband. 'What about the voice, for instance?'

'There'd have been no problem about that, at least. According to Band, it's well-known that all the Postons shared a distinctively similar tone of voice.'

'But still an awful lot of people must have been in the know.'

'Not necessarily as many as all that. Diana, of course, and her brother Guy. Not, I think, young Celia, though it must have been hard to keep it from her.' Thorne was ticking off names on his fingers. 'Tony Dinsley, almost certainly. Frank Leder, but I suspect not his wife. If I'm right that could make five, with Henry himself.'

'But what about old Sir Oliver and the people at the manor? And Alan's friends and acquaintances?'

'Sir Oliver was almost blind. Alan didn't visit him very often, which meant that the Harmans wouldn't know him well because they hadn't been there long. Tom Calindar was different. I think he was killed because he began to think something was wrong. He may not have known exactly what, but he could have suspected Henry. Maybe that's what he intended to tell Band. The odd thing is that he left it so long. Why didn't he start to have his doubts sooner? We can only assume they took steps to avoid him. And of course one sees what one expects to see. That would have gone for Alan's friends. And the need for Alan to stay quiet after his accident would have been a good excuse for keeping even those away. In any case, there's no reason why they shouldn't have accepted the new Alan—especially with his head bandaged and his hair shaved and all that.'

It was a long speech for George Thorne, and Miranda considered it carefully. Then she said, 'Nancy Naury must have been a shock to them.'

'Yes.' Thorne nodded, his expression suddenly sombre. 'I hadn't forgotten. I may have uncovered a neat little fraud, but I've still got to find a multiple murderer.'

Not long after breakfast the following morning the new houseman at the manor drew Alan Poston aside and said quietly, 'Sir, a lady telephoned. A Miss Joy Saint. Would you call her at the Randolph Hotel as soon as possible. She told me to say it was vitally important, but she wouldn't let me get you there and then. She wanted me to pass the message—er—discreetly, as it were, sir.'

'Oh. I see. Yes, thanks.'

It seemed a suitable moment. No one was around. Guy had gone up to London, Tony to Oxford, the women weren't in evidence. Alan Poston put through the call at once. Miss Saint was obviously waiting to hear from him, and she wasted no time over niceties.

She said, 'I told your butler, or whoever he was, to catch you when you were alone. Does anyone else know you're calling me?'

'No, but—'

'Good. I want to see you. Be here at the Randolph. In an hour.'

'I—I don't know if I—'

'An hour, Henry, and by yourself. Not with your wife, or any of those pals of yours. Not unless you want big trouble.'

Coming from Joy Saint, the threat was enough. Alan Poston left the manor almost immediately, and only Celia saw him depart. He drove fast, too fast, but he arrived in Oxford without mishap, parked the car and made for the hotel.

Joy Saint was sitting at the far end of the big lounge. She got to her feet as he hurried across the room towards her, smiling what he hoped was a pleasant greeting. Miss Saint ignored his outstretched hand. Instead, she nodded towards the man who had appeared behind him.

'Mr Poston?'

He whipped round. 'Who—Oh, it's you,' he said as he saw Thorne, his smile fading. 'What is it?' He turned back to Joy Saint. 'You arranged this!' he said accusingly. 'Getting me here under false pretences!'

She looked at him without speaking, turned her back and walked away. Alan Poston swallowed hard. He tried to grin at the Superintendent, but it wasn't much of a success.

'Damn women!' he said.

'Mr Poston, I'd like you to come with me to my headquarters at Bicester. I've got a car outside.'

'Why? More of your bloody questions, I suppose. What if I refuse?'

'Your refusal would be noted, sir. But I think you'd be ill-advised.'

For a second the two men regarded each other, but the outcome was never in doubt. Poston dropped his gaze, mumbled something that Thorne didn't catch and shrugged.

'Okay, then. What are we waiting for?'

The drive to Bicester was silent, except for a murmur to Sergeant Abbot who was waiting with the unmarked police car. Thorne sat in front with his sergeant, and discour-

aged any further attempt at conversation. He wanted to give
the man time to stew, to appreciate his position. But, once
they were all three settled in Thorne's office, the questions
came thick and fast.

Poston admitted he'd had an affair with Nancy Naury.
His wife had learnt of it, but they'd been going their own
ways for a long time and she hadn't given a damn. He'd
taken the name Henry Logan to deceive Nancy rather than
his wife; ex-girlfriends could become a nuisance. Anyway,
he couldn't see where the police came in. 'I can call myself
anything I like,' he said.

'And you had no idea there was such a person as Henry
Logan?'

'No. Why should I care if there was—is? I might have
called myself John Smith. Is this Logan going to sue me for
using his name?' He made the question sound facetious.
The interview was going well from his point of view. 'My
God, is that what all the fuss is about?'

'No, sir. I'm afraid not. It's about murder.'

'Murder!'

The silence lengthened as the atmosphere in the room
changed. The Superintendent's smile became almost benign
as he stroked his moustache. Abbot found himself holding
his breath.

'The murder of Alan Poston,' Thorne said at length, quite
quietly.

'Alan Poston? Murder? But—but—I'm Alan Poston.'

'Sir, I'm about to give you the official warning,' Thorne
said, aware from Abbot's anxious coughs that he was thinking it was high time to formalize the interrogation. 'Then I
shall ask you to make a statement. Before I do, however, I
should tell you that when this Henry Logan, of whom you've
never heard, was in Australia he got into a spot of trouble
with the police. An efficient lot—the Sydney force. They
keep excellent records. It took them no time to look up
Henry Logan's fingerprints. They're on their way here now

by facsimile, if they haven't already arrived.'

Again there was a heavy silence. Poston had started to sweat. There were beads of moisture on his brow and above his lip. But his mouth seemed to be dry because he kept swallowing and trying to moisten his lips with his tongue. Beneath his tan, his complexion had become pale.

'It—it was an accident,' he said at last. 'That's what Diana told me. I wasn't even there—if you know so much, you must know I wasn't. I've—I've never killed anyone.'

'But you are Henry Logan, sir? Not Alan Poston?'

'Yes,' he nodded reluctantly.

'Then perhaps you should begin your statement, Mr Logan.'

Henry Logan's statement held very few surprises for Superintendent Thorne.

Henry had met Alan and Diana Poston quite by chance some eighteen months ago, shortly after his return from Australia. He had gatecrashed a party in London and Diana had spotted him across a crowded room. The likeness between the two men had delighted the Postons. Everyone was supposed to have a double, and here in the flesh was Alan's. There was no reason to believe they were related, even distantly.

'Of course, we didn't look so much alike then,' Logan said. 'My hair was lighter, for one thing—it's dyed now— and I didn't brush my eyebrows upwards in this extraordinary fashion, and I was a good deal thinner. Still—'

Logan had seen a certain amount of the Postons, and then they had left on one of their trips abroad. But Diana had said keep in touch and, when he'd moved in with Nancy Naury, he'd sent them his phone number. He'd heard nothing from them till Diana called him very early in the morning of August 10th.

'She asked—bluntly, just like that—if I wanted to make half a million for a few months' work and I said, who wouldn't? We met at her flat later in the morning, and she told me Alan had killed himself in an accident and that my job would be to impersonate him till the old man was dead and his fortune parcelled out.'

Logan had agreed. He'd put himself entirely in Diana Poston's hands, and that day in London she'd immediately started to coach him in his part. Later when he was confined to his room at the lodge as Alan, the other three in the plot —Guy Frint, Tony Dinsley and Frank Leder—had taken their turns. The accident, especially an accident involving potential concussion, had excused any slight changes in appearance and behaviour—and even in his signature.

There had been difficulties, of course. The dog had been a blasted nuisance; it hadn't liked him and had howled for its master. Then there had been Celia. Luckily she'd never been close to Alan, and Diana had packed her off to France as soon as possible. After that, it had largely been a question of avoiding people who'd known Alan at all well. But there was always the accident to provide an excuse for a quiet life.

'It wasn't too bad at first,' Logan said with apparent candour. 'By my standards we were living luxuriously, but the old man took a long time to die, and things— relationships—got strained. It was a relief when Sir Oliver went—and when Tom Calindar went so soon afterwards. Calindar had been giving me some funny looks. But I didn't kill any of them, Superintendent, I swear it. I've never killed anyone. Maybe someone did. Kill them I mean—Alan and the old man and Calindar—and Leder for that matter. Maybe someone thought Nancy was a threat and arranged that car crash. But it wasn't me. I knew nothing about any of it. I just went on pretending to be Alan.'

Logan put his head between his arms on the desk in front of him and began to sob silently. He looked up at Thorne. 'Enough,' he said. 'I've told you all I can. I'm exhausted. Charge me with fraud or anything you like, except murder.

Then put me in a cell. Don't send me back to the manor.'

Thorne and Abbot had left him soon after that, sipping at a mug of strong tea, a constable in charge. 'Do you believe him, sir?' Abbot had said as they walked along towards the cafeteria.

Without hesitation Thorne said, 'Yes, I believe him. He's no murderer. But one of the others is—or more if there was a conspiracy. We must pull them in before anything else happens.'

CHAPTER 23

Henry Logan was left to languish in an interview room with a constable to keep him company while Superintendent Thorne saw the Chief Constable. Thorne was anxious that his suspects should be picked up simultaneously as far as possible, or at least that every effort should be made to stop them communicating with each other once they were in the hands of the police and 'helping with inquiries'. To this end, an extensive and fairly successful operation was rapidly mounted.

By early in the afternoon Tony Dinsley had been found at his Oxford college, while Diana and Celia had been brought from the manor. Guy had been to his London flat, according to the porter, but had left again. He was expected to return to the manor later in the day, and discreet surveillance of the house was ordered. If the Met didn't find Guy, it was hoped to pick him up when he got home.

The Superintendent elected to interview Celia first. When a WPC had brought her to his office, he tried to put her at her ease by asking if she'd had time for any lunch.

Celia was obviously surprised and a little nervous at the situation. It was, after all, the only genuine brush with the police she had faced in her young life, but she answered quite calmly, 'Yes, thank you. We'd just finished when—when—'

'Good. Would you like some coffee, then?' And when Celia shook her head. 'Please don't be alarmed, Miss Frint. I don't believe you've broken the law in any way, but I do think you may have some information that can help us.'

'What about?' Celia asked tentatively.

'Alan Poston. Your half-sister's husband.'

'Alan? Has Alan—done something?'

Thorne ignored the question. 'Miss Frint,' he said quietly, 'to begin with I want you to cast your mind back to the night of Mr Poston's accident last year, and tell us how it happened.'

'I don't really know,' Celia said at once. 'I wasn't there. I'd gone to bed.'

'So I gather, Miss Frint. But just tell us what you saw or heard that night and the day after.'

Celia knitted her brows. She had had no opportunity to speak to Diana when the police arrived at the manor, nor in the car during the drive to Bicester and since their arrival here they had been kept in separate rooms. She was perturbed. She didn't understand what was happening, but she saw no reason for refusing the Superintendent's request. Prompted at intervals by Thorne, she described the events of that night and the following day as she remembered them.

'So you and Mr Dinsley spent the afternoon in Oxford and arrived back too late to see Mr Poston. When did you get to see him?'

'The next day, after lunch. Diana said he needed complete rest and was kicking us all out of the house. I was to go up to London to stay with Guy, and then to France sooner than I'd expected. But I did look into Alan's room to say goodbye to him. His head was all bandaged and he was half asleep.'

'I see,' said Thorne. 'So you had no real contact with him at that time. And the next time you saw him must have been when you came home for Sir Oliver's funeral?'

Celia's eyes widened. 'That's right. But how—how do you know all this about us?'

Again Thorne ignored Celia's question. 'And at the time of the funeral—did he strike you as different in any way?'

'Different? Different—how do you mean?'

'Well, did you think the accident—the head injury—had affected him? Did he seem the same Alan you'd known before you were packed off to France—' Thorne paused; he couldn't lead his witness too fast or too far.

Celia paused too, hesitating before she replied. 'Yes, I did,' she said finally. 'He was always a bit odd but now sometimes I thought he was really going round the bend. I even told Dr Band about it. As you say, it must have been the bang on his head.'

She told the Superintendent of Alan Poston's food poisoning, and how she'd had to call Dr Band, and had told the doctor about the unexpected pass Alan had made at her after Sir Oliver's funeral. She mentioned Nelson, and Alan's unusual difficulties in the pool. Thorne of course had heard it all before, but he listened politely. When she stopped speaking, he said, 'Ah yes, the dog Nelson, Miss Frint. You were fond of him?'

Thorne had intended this as a throwaway question, meant to reassure the girl and end the interview pleasantly. By now he was convinced that she was totally innocent of any crime, and he could only feel sorry for her. Innocent or not, she was going to have a bad time when the case became public knowledge. But Celia's reply surprised him.

'Yes, he was a dear,' Celia said. 'Mind you, he was a one-man dog. He adored Alan and only made do with other people. It was awful he should have been put down, and it was all my fault. If I'd not let him out he'd never have gone digging up the compost heap, or bitten Tony when he tried to catch him.'

'Digging up the compost heap.' It cost Thorne an effort to keep the excitement from his voice and sound merely amused. 'And was that one of his favourite places?'

'Oh no,' said Celia. 'At least, I'd never seen him digging there before.'

By now Thorne was on his feet, suggesting that the WPC should take Celia to the canteen for a while, but drawing her aside and asking her to find out tactfully if the girl had any relations or friends she could go to later. Abbot had already disappeared. A nod from his superior had been enough to tell him what action to take—and urgent action too.

Abbot returned as Diana Poston was being shown into Thorne's office by another WPC. Diana was calm but tense as she took a seat in front of the Superintendent's desk. His hope was to shock her into some disclosure.

As she opened her mouth to utter the expected protest, he said, 'Mrs Poston, you've been brought here because we're hoping you can help us. We have reason to believe that on the night of ninth to tenth of August last year your husband was murdered.'

Diana's half-open mouth shut suddenly. She turned, to look out of the window, to glance at Sergeant Abbot and at the WPC sitting quietly in the background, before she replied to the Superintendent.

'Murdered? Alan? You must be joking!' She stood up. 'I think I'll leave now. Please arrange to have me escorted to my home. I shall make a formal protest about the incredible treatment I've received at the hands of the police.'

'Incredible treatment, Mrs Poston?' Thorne was at his blandest. 'I'm sure no one's been subjecting you to any form of torture—not here in Bicester.' He grinned suddenly. 'Now, about this murder. My information comes from Mr Henry Logan.'

There was a pause. These interviews seemed to be punctuated by pregnant pauses, Thorne thought unoriginally. Diana stared at the floor. She was clearly under stress, hands clenched, neck stiff. Thorne thought the best course would be to shock her further with an official caution, but she interrupted him.

'I refuse to answer any further questions,' she said firmly. 'I know my rights. I demand to speak to my solicitor and have him present at any future interviews.'

At this stage, Thorne was not prepared to make an issue of Diana's demand. He merely bowed his head in agreement and watched speculatively as the WPC led her from the room. 'She's tough, that one,' he said.

'But could she have done it, sir?' said Abbot.

'What do you think? It's possible. Or she may have had help. We'll see what her boyfriend has to say. Go and get Dinsley, Abbot. Let's hope he'll talk.'

Thorne was rapidly losing patience, and bluntly faced Tony Dinsley with a possible charge of murder. So Tony Dinsley did talk. From him for the first time, the Superintendent heard an eye-witness account of Alan Poston's death and its immediate aftermath.

Dinsley swore that the whole thing had started with a genuine accident. 'Why should we have killed him?' he demanded. 'We wanted him alive—we needed him alive— if Diana was to get her hands on any of old Sir Oliver's money. That's all we wanted—the money.'

'I'm quite aware of that, Mr Dinsley.' said Thorne. 'But did you want it enough to hasten Sir Oliver's death?'

Dinsley stared at him. 'First Alan! Now the old man! You must be obsessed with murder, Superintendent. I repeat, Alan death's was an accident. We were all horrified when it happened. Then Di remember this chap Logan—and the whole thing developed from there. The plan was quite simple. Di hurried off to London and put it to Logan. Once he'd agreed, I took Celia to Oxford and kept her out of the way while Guy buried the body in the garden.' Dinsley laughed uncertainly. 'He wasn't used to such hard labour. He blistered his hands so badly he had to tell Celia he'd burnt them on the stove.'

Then he became serious again. 'I suppose that was when we were really committed. I realize what we did was criminal—concealing a death, intention to defraud, God knows what else—but murder, no!'

Tony Dinsley was emphatic. All his high hopes of academic or political advancement were shattered. Instead, he saw little chance of avoiding a prison sentence. How long a sentence would depend on how good a barrister he could afford, how lenient the judge. He might get away with two or three years if he were in the least lucky. But a charge of murder or being an accessory to murder was a different matter. He was appalled at the prospect.

For his part, George Thorne was also unhappy. Almost against his will he believed that Dinsley was telling the truth, that Alan Poston's death had in fact been accidental. And his residual doubts about his whole hypothesis were beginning to reassert themselves. All the other fatalities— Sir Oliver, Tom Calindar, Frank Leder—could also have been innocent and coincidental, and so could Nancy Naury's crash. Evidence to the contrary was meagre and would never stand up in court. Not that the DPP would let it get so far.

Thorne said, 'Tell me, sir, what was to happen once the supposed Alan Poston was in possession of the residue of Sir Oliver's estate?'

Dinsley couldn't see that at this stage he had anything to lose from cooperating; at least wholehearted cooperation might gain him some police goodwill. 'Broadly speaking,' he said, 'Alan was to settle it on Diana, keeping half a million for himself. Guy Frint, Frank Leder and I were to get half a million each. Then Diana was to divorce Alan, who'd go abroad for a bit and return to being Henry Logan.' He raised his eyes to the Superintendent's. 'I said it was a simple plan.'

'It was certainly convenient.' Thorne was brusque. 'And after all that I assume you proposed to marry Mrs Poston, which means that the two of you had easily the most to gain.'

'Yes, but—'

'Leder's death saved you half a million, it seems. Who was to go next, Mr Dinsley? Guy Frint? Or the pseudo Alan? And once you were married was the new Mrs Dinsley to have an unfortunate accident?' Thorne knew he was pressing much too hard, but he could see no alternative if this interview was to lead anywhere useful.

But Dinsley's reactions remained unhelpful. He merely said, 'No, Superintendent, you're quite wrong. You're seeing things that don't exist, inventing possibilities and calling them reality.'

'What about Henry Logan? He maintains you'd have drowned him if Celia Frint hadn't come on the scene. When that failed, did you try poison, sir? Mr Logan was very ill.'

'No, Superintendent.' Tony Dinsley was quite calm now, and completely acquiescent. 'You've got it all wrong, as I say. Let me explain a bit more.'

Thorne nodded, and Dinsley told how Henry Logan had become difficult. As a result of Sir Oliver's will he had learnt that his mother had been the old man's mistress and realized that his likeness to Alan was no accident. He, too, was a son of Sir Oliver's, and as such he claimed he should have a larger share of the estate. They'd argued about it. By now tempers were becoming thin, as they realized their dependence on each other.

'I admit I thought I might give Logan a fright, bring him to his senses, show him how vulnerable he was,' Dinsley said. 'But I deny absolutely that I intended to drown him. I doubt if I could have. He's a much bigger man than me. In fact, he'd kicked me in the eye and surfaced by the time Celia got to the pool.'

'And what about the so-called food poisoning?' Thorne demanded.

Dinsley shook his head wearily. 'God knows. I don't. I expect it really was food poisoning.'

'Another accident?' Thorne said sarcastically. Then abruptly he asked, 'Do you keep a diary—an engagement book, Mr Dinsley?'

'Yes. Why?'

Thorne held out his hand without speaking, and Dinsley produced a diary from an inside pocket of his jacket. It was a slim book, leather-covered, gold-edged, with his initials gold-blocked in one corner. Thorne leafed through it quickly.

He was of course mainly interested in three dates: the night of Sir Oliver's death, the night of his funeral when Tom Calindar had died, and the evening of Frank Leder's death. In the diary in the spaces allocated to the first two dates were the words, 'Di. Lodge.', just as he'd expected. Against the date of Leder's death the book read, 'Drinks 6. Master. Dinner in hall', and the name of a junior cabinet minister.

Thorne turned the diary around so that Dinsley could read this entry. 'What does that mean?' he said.

Dinsley frowned. 'That? Just what it says. The minister, who happens to be both a member of my college and a friend, came down to Oxford for the night. We had drinks with the Master in his Lodgings, then dinner in hall and a good gossip afterwards in my rooms. But what—'

'Thank you,' Thorne said. 'Thank you, sir. That will be all for now. Sergeant Abbot will arrange for you to have some tea while your statement's being typed.'

Nodding his dismissal, the Superintendent immersed himself in the papers in front of him, while Abbot led an oddly reluctant Dinsley from the room. As the door closed behind him, Thorne abandoned his act and permitted himself a long sigh. Perhaps, he thought, Dinsley was right, and he was becoming obsessed with the idea of multiple murder. With the exception of young Celia, they were a pretty unpleasant crowd, but that didn't mean they were prepared to kill. Nevertheless, he told himself, the whole thing still stank.

He was pacing up and down his office when Abbot returned. 'Any news?' he asked at once.

'No, sir. They've almost reached ground level at the bottom of the compost heap, but no sign of a body yet. They're going on digging.'

Thorne grunted. 'What about Frint? He's the one who's supposed to have buried it.'

'Nothing so far, sir.'

'Okay.' Thorne made up his mind. 'You stay here and hold the fort, Abbot. I'll drive myself over to the lodge. If Frint turns up, hang on to him. Hang on to all of them. I'll keep in touch.'

'Yes, sir,' Abbot said, and thought he'd better phone his current girlfriend and tell her there was no hope of a disco that night.

CHAPTER 24

Detective-Superintendent Thorne was a very self-controlled character. In spite of his inner tension he was able to drive fast, but without letting his concentration waver. His virtue was rewarded; it saved him from what might have been a nasty accident.

He was within fifty yards of the entrance to the manor driveway when a small red BMW backed out at speed, turned and hurtled directly towards him. The road at this point was just wide enough for two cars, and it was only at the last moment that the driver of the BMW seemed to realize Thorne's presence and make any effort to get off the crown of the road. In the meantime, Thorne's reactions had been fast. He pushed his foot hard down on the brake and drove deliberately into the hedge on his near side.

The BMW swerved past him, and he had only a glimpse of the driver, not enough to recognize whoever it might be. A uniformed police officer had come running out of the driveway in obviously futile pursuit. Thorne undid his seatbelt and climbed out of his listing car on to the road.

'Are you all right, sir?' It was Sergeant Court, out of breath.

'Yes, I'm all right, Sergeant. Was that maniac the man I think it was?'

'It was Mr Frint, sir. He must have seen the police vehicles in front of the lodge and made off as quick as he could.'

'I see,' Thorne said shortly.

Indeed, as he came to the entrance to the driveway he saw only too well. The police presence was ridiculously obvious. Two marked police cars and a van were lined up in the drive. A police dog, an officer holding his leash, was lifting his leg against a nearby tree. And from behind the lodge came shouts of encouragement as those who were taking a break urged on those who were digging.

No wonder Frint had fled, Thorne thought bitterly, disgusted with himself for not having made it clear to Abbot that the search should be conducted as unobtrusively as possible. Doubtless there was another police car up at the manor and a couple of officers waiting for Frint there, but all this activity had provided him with an unmistakably early warning. Lack of foresight meant that they would now have no alternative but to face the dreary routine of a nationwide hunt.

'I'll use your radio, Sergeant,' Thorne said sharply. 'Get one of your men to put my car back on the road. I guess it's only scratched.'

'Yes, sir!'

While the Sergeant hurried off, Thorne got himself

patched through to Abbot. He wasted no time in recrimi-
nations, but described Guy Frint's vehicle, told Abbot to
get a description of the man from Celia, and make arrangements to detain him when he was traced. 'And don't forget
the ports and airports,' he added for good measure.

Abbot said, 'He's our man, you think, sir?'

Thorne cut him short. 'He's bolted, hasn't he? He's got
something on his conscience. But what? Fraud? Concealing
a death? Murder? How the hell do I know? Get on with it,
Sergeant, and don't ask silly questions. No! Wait! Get things
started on another phone, but stay on this line!'

While Thorne had been speaking the shouting from the
garden had been replaced by a sudden silence. It was
clear that something had been found. Thorne put down the
microphone and walked round the lodge with long, quick
strides.

He found Sergeant Court and five uniformed men in their
shirtsleeves, leaning on their spaces and staring down at a
shallow grave beside a pile of compost. A blanketed bundle
lay in the earth, and the stench was appalling. It was not
surprising that one of the younger men made a sudden dash
for the bushes and was violently sick. Thorne and the others
took out handkerchiefs and bound them round their noses
and mouths to give themselves some protection.

Thorne bent over the bundle, holding his breath, and
gave it the briefest of examinations, disturbing it as little as
possible.

'Okay. It's a body,' he said. 'Sergeant Court, Abbot's still
on the radio. Tell him to get the team here as soon as
possible. And the pathologist, too. And get Dr Band, if you
can.'

'Yes, sir.'

Thorne turned to the other officers. 'As long as someone
stays where he can keep an eye on the hole, we can find
some fresh air. Not a nice job,' he added.

'No, sir,' said one of the men as they moved away. 'But

at least we didn't have to dig up the whole garden. I gather some dog told us where to look first.'

Thorne nodded thoughtfully.

An hour later the investigation was proceeding under reasonable control. Photographs and measurements had been taken, and the bundle carefully lifted from its makeshift grave and laid on the grass. Dr Band and the pathologist, who had arrived on the scene at much the same time, had completed a preliminary examination, and the pathologist, in a hurry as always, had departed, leaving Band to report to the Superintendent.

'There's not much we can tell you,' Band said. 'It's the partially decomposed body of a male, a big man nearing middle age, dead about a year. He's had an almighty whack on the head, but no one'll know if that was the immediate cause of death till after the post morten, if then. Personally, I've got a feeling the body's vaguely familiar.'

Thorne grinned. 'So it should be,' he said. 'It's Alan Poston. He died on the tenth of August last year, after his fortieth birthday party, and almost certainly from that whack on the head.'

'But then who—' Band began.

'Chap called Henry Logan, Poston's half-brother, but keep that under your hat for the moment. I must be off now. Thanks a lot. See you soon.' Thorne turned to go, then turned back. 'Incidentally,' he added, 'an awful lot may depend on the exact cause of that cracked head.'

Guy Frint was waiting for Thorne on his return to Bicester. For once the police had had a stroke of luck and a couple of traffic officers had stopped a BMW for speeding. They had just asked for Frint's licence when the radio call came through. Frint had offered no resistance.

Now he sat across the desk from the Superintendent, outwardly calm. Only an intermittent tick at the corner of

his mouth suggested that he was under any stress. To
Abbot's relief, Thorne cautioned him immediately.

'So what?' Guy asked, with apparent calm. 'What am I
supposed to have done?'

'We've not yet completed the formulation of the precise
charges,' Thorne said airily. 'But doubtless they'll include
failure to notify a death, intent to defraud, accessory to a
criminal impersonation. And, of course, murder—the murder of Alan Poston. That should be enough to go on with.'

After a long minute, Frint said, 'Not guilty.'

'Do you deny that you were present at Alan Poston's
house, known as The Lodge, on the night of ninth to tenth
of August last year with your sister, Diana Poston?'

'No, I was there.'

'So you admit you were present when Alan Poston was
killed? You must realize, Mr Frint, that therefore you are,
if not the actual murderer, at least an accessory before and
after the fact, just like Diana Poston and Celia—'

'No one killed Alan. It was an accident. He was drunk
and he fell and cracked his head on a stone step.'

'That'll be very difficult to prove now that the body's
spent a year under a compost heap—where you buried him,
Mr Frint.'

'The others—'

'What others, Mr Frint? Your sister and her lover? Your
young half-sister?'

'Celia was in bed. She knew nothing.'

Superintendent Thorne ignored the comment. 'There was
Frank Leder, of course, but he's dead. Anyway, he'd hardly
be an impartial witness. Admittedly Henry Logan says it
was an accident, but he wasn't there. He only knows what
he was told.'

'But it doesn't make sense. If you know as much as I
guess you do, you must be able to see that. Why should I
—any of us—have wanted to kill Alan? All we wanted was
Alan alive.'

Thorne said, 'Let me put something to you, Mr Frint. Suppose Alan Poston had become fed up with the whole lot of you. He wasn't a fool. Suppose he knew his wife was only waiting for Sir Oliver to die and for him to inherit before divorcing him, claiming a huge settlement and marrying— or not marrying—Tony Dinsley. Suppose he himself had decided to forestall this by divorcing Diana—God knows he had enough grounds—and thus get rid of all of you. What might you have done then? You could have formed a conspiracy to kill him, and substitute Henry Logan in his place. Probably Poston did fall and knock himself out. But you—one or all of you—finished him off.' Thorne was smiling. 'How does that strike you as a valid explanation of events, Mr Frint?'

Guy Frint stared at the Superintendent with dawning understanding. Thorne's sardonic smile and the hint of amusement in his voice told their own story. The police were playing with him.

'It's not true,' he said. 'None of it's true. And you don't even believe it yourself.'

'It doesn't matter what I believe, Mr Frint. It's what the judge and the jury will believe that matters. And the prosecution will have an excellent case, I assure you. I'd predict a life sentence for you, fifteen years for Diana, ten —perhaps less—for Celia, considering her youth.'

'You—you bugger? I always knew the police were a filthy lot, but you—'

Frint thrust back his chair and launched himself across the desk at Thorne, seizing him by the throat. Luckily for his superior, Abbot, who had given up any pretence of taking notes, was watching Frint's reactions closely and had to some extent anticipated such an attack. He leapt on Frint and banged his head down on the desk, making him release the Superintendent.

Two minutes later, peace restored, Thorne continued his interrogation. 'Let's assume for the sake of argument that

Alan Poston's death *was* an accident, and nothing but an accident,' he said, 'and that it was witnessed by Diana Poston—there's no gainsaying that—but not by Celia, who accepted Henry Logan as Alan. Then your sentence, and Diana's, would be greatly reduced. Celia, of course, wouldn't be charged at all.'

'That's what happened, and you know it,' Frint said grimly.

'I might be prepared to accept it,' Thorne admitted, 'but for one thing. The police like to bring criminals to justice, Mr Frint, especially those who murder for the sake of gain. I believe you killed Tom Calindar because he suspected that Henry Logan was an impostor. But I'll be honest with you. There's not enough evidence to make a case. So I'll have to get you over Alan Poston, with the obviously unpleasant consequences for your family. Unless—' Thorne waited.

'—unless I confess? I was right,' Frint said thickly. 'You are a bugger, Superintendent.' He sat silent for a while. Then he shrugged. 'But okay. You win.'

'I've never been so relieved in my life,' George Thorne admitted to his wife when he got home very late, the formalities completed and all his prisoners safe in cells for the night. In response to Miranda's eager questions, he explained that it had been decided to charge Guy Frint with murder and attempted murder, and Diana Poston, Logan and Dinsley with concealing a body and fraud and so on. It was accepted that Celia knew nothing about any of it, and she had been released. In court in the morning the magistrates would be asked to remand Frint in custody, but allow the others bail.

'But if Frint had dug in his heels I'd have been stumped,' Thorne added ruefully. 'I'd never have made a charge of killing Poston stick. In fact, I'm prepared to accept that his was the one death that wasn't murder. There was no conceivable motive.'

'You certainly took a chance,' Miranda said. 'It was nothing but blackmail on your part. Suppose he'd not cared about Diana or Celia?'

'It may have been blackmail, but it was justice too,' Thorne said stoutly. 'You should read his statement. Once Frint started to tell all, nothing stopped him. He admits to smothering Sir Oliver because the old man took too long to die. He admits to pushing Calindar down the cellar steps because they thought Sir Oliver's old servant was beginning to realize that Logan was a phoney; apparently Diana noticed things. She thought Calindar was behaving oddly, and once Logan refused some anchovies Calindar was offering him, saying he couldn't stand them. Calindar would know quite well they were a passion of the real Alan's.'

'And Leder?'

'Oh, Frint admits he poisoned Frank Leder because Leder was becoming importunate, as he puts it. He admits to making Logan sick to stop him going to London. He says he used disulfiram—that stuff that makes you sick if you touch alcohol; it's a prescription drug, but quite easy to get hold of. As for Nancy Naury's crash, he was responsible for that too. He'd been practising throwing stones on that corner just in case he needed to get rid of Logan eventually.'

'If Alan Poston's death was really an accident, the whole affair seems to have been a case of one thing leading to another,' Miranda said.

'Yes, that's true. But don't forget there was always a driving force—greed. Frint was very close to Diana. He hoped to get a good deal more from her than a mere half million. He's been doing less well with his gambling recently, and he had some debts. But it wasn't so much that he needed money urgently. What he wanted was to be really rich, to be able to gamble on a large scale, not to have to bother ever again about where the next penny or pound or thousand was coming from.' Thorne smothered a yawn. 'For that matter, it was greed that drove them all—including, I suspect, poor Nancy Naury. She's going to live, it seems, but I wonder if she'll wait for her Henry to come out of gaol when she discovers he's penniless.'

'Don't be so cynical, George,' Miranda said, mild reproof in her voice. 'What put you on to Guy, rather than Diana or Dinsley, or a genuine conspiracy?'

'Hardly great detective work, my love. Elimination, really. Dinsley had an alibi for the time of Leder's death, and in my judgement he was too astute to enter into the conspiracy. I hesitated over Guy and Diana; as I said, they've been very close all their lives—even Diana's original meeting with Alan apparently resulted from a kind of minor conspiratorial ploy arranged between them. I could see them acting in concert. But I wasn't getting anywhere with Diana and in the end Guy solved the problem by taking to his heels—or wheels, you might say. If she has enough sense to keep quiet I don't think we'll ever know the true extent of Diana's involvement. And I'm not sure it matters all that much.'

'I see,' said Miranda thoughtfully. 'And what about Celia? You said she'd been released, but how will all this affect her?'

'She's staying with the Bands for the moment, as she's no relations, and she's pretty miserable, Band tells me. The only thing she's happy about is that the dog Nelson wasn't put down. She says she wants to see Basil Kale to thank him. She had no part in any crime, so when she's twenty-one she'll get the money Sir Oliver left her, and the lawyers can easily arrange for her to borrow on it before that. Let's hope she'll be happy.' He paused, and stared at his wife. 'Not a very satisfactory case on the whole,' he concluded. 'But they'll all get their deserts, I hope.'

Then, though he did his best, Thorne couldn't hide his yawns and Miranda took the hint. 'Come on, love,' she said. 'You've done your bit. Forget it for now. Bed.'

John Penn, a pseudonym, is the author of *An Ad for Murder, Stag Dinner Death, A Will to Kill,* and *Mortal Term.*